George Lansing Taylor

Elijah the Reformer

A Ballad Epic, and Other Sacred and Religious Poems. Second Edition

George Lansing Taylor

Elijah the Reformer
A Ballad Epic, and Other Sacred and Religious Poems. Second Edition

ISBN/EAN: 9783744783989

Printed in Europe, USA, Canada, Australia, Japan

Cover: Foto ©Andreas Hilbeck / pixelio.de

More available books at **www.hansebooks.com**

Elijah the Reformer

A BALLAD-EPIC

AND OTHER

SACRED AND RELIGIOUS POEMS

BY

GEO. LANSING TAYLOR, D.D.

Second Edition.

FUNK & WAGNALLS

NEW YORK
10 AND 12 DEY STREET

1885

LONDON
44 FLEET STREET

DEDICATION.

My Revered Mother : You have passed the allotted " three-score years and ten" of mortal life, and are now pressing on toward " fourscore."

My first remembrance of you is the picture of a blooming young woman, who, having taught me to read fluently before I can remember, was then teaching me orally, from her own memory, many of the best old nursery ballads of the English tongue, until I should be old enough to lawfully attempt the ambitions of a country schoolhouse.

Those ballads, always of a serious tinge, were often of a weird and somber rhythm, and produced a profound impression on a mind no doubt hereditarily predisposed to their influence. The vibrating memory of those haunting cadences, and the conversational Bible-readings and hymns of my father at the family altar, were the loom in which the spell was woven which, from childhood, drew my mind to the marvels of sacred story and the witchery of sacred numbers. Stronger, even, than the fascination of my boyhood's thrice-read Rollin and Buffon and Milton and Bunyan was, and ever will be, that of the wonders of God's work in Old Testament history, and the fire of Old Testament song.

But to you is directly traceable much of that fascination, for to you, and with your explanations, I read aloud those wonders and songs, as the reading lessons and devotional exercises of my earliest childhood.

It is therefore only a small sheaf of your own sowing which I dutifully lay at your feet to-day, in this collected volume of sacred poems ; and I am thankful that you yet linger in the " Land of Beulah" to receive them, and to bestow your latest blessing on the gleaner, before passing on to rejoin him who, among the " spirits of just men made perfect," awaits you on the brighter shore.

Several of these pieces you have seen, in their fugitive forms, as printed years ago. If I have been slow in gathering them into the bundle of a volume, let the explanation here also be your own influence—namely, the early lesson of painstaking thoroughness, which taught me to consider no work finished while it was in my power to make it better. And this also is why some of them have lain from fifteen to twenty-five years in manuscript, going through several carefully written editions, before being offered for types.

And now, having been first moved by your spirit, and then having striven to obey your precept, I humbly offer you this belated first-fruits sheaf, earnestly wishing it were worthier of your approval.

PREFACE.

THE poems composing this volume, except in the case of the "Elijah," which is now for the first time printed entire, are selections from the author's miscellaneous pieces, old and new, which, by the indulgence of sundry kind-hearted editors, have appeared in magazines and newspapers during the last twenty-five years. They have been selected so as to form a volume of religious poems, which should have (except in the position of the leading poem) the progressive order of history in the biblical pieces and that of religious thought in the others.

A word as to the pieces themselves. Heroic epic poems are rarer than century plants. They bloom not by centuries, but one for each great national civilization, and only one. But the minor epic, the narrative ballad, will always be written as the poem of the people. The "Elijah" of this volume, although treating of the sublimest hero and moral epopee of the prophetic dispensation, and lifting into vision not only the hero, but (by the poetic license of anachronism) the whole age affected by his ministry, is not an attempt at heroic epic, but only at ballad epic; although developed, as I believe, beyond any previous model of the ballad. The other biblical pieces are mainly ballads, epical in substance and spirit, but the humbler and more popular ballad in form. In the only formal ode inserted, "The Prophecy of Wisdom," I have taken the liberty to make a wide departure from the rule of Archilochus, the inventor of the ode, and to introduce five antistrophes instead of one, between the strophe and the epode, in order that I might introduce all the personified characters necessary to my plan, with their claims, before the epode (which I have lengthened) sums up and answers to the strophe, to close the ode.

Perhaps the author is indebted to a sort of compulsion

for the courage to offer even this volume to the public.
John Wesley, in the preface to the second volume of his sermons
(which had been printed currently in the *Arminian Magazine*),
says he found that another clergyman was about to print them
in a volume, on which he quaintly, but sensibly, remarks : " If
it must be done, . . . methinks I am the properest person to
do it." So, when prominent publishers are using the imper-
fect forms of these pieces without compensation to the author
(over thirty pieces or extracts in one work), the author has no
choice but to shock up his sheaves, or else have his little harvest go into other barns than his own. He has therefore collected and carefully revised these poems, and now transfers
them to his publishers in their only authorized forms. If, on
the grounds of competent literary criticism, they shall receive
a small share of the favor that has thus far been extended to
them by a very lenient religious public, the author will be
thankful. He has not attempted to follow the canons of
æsthetic art, which would conceal the moral in the texture of
the work, or else suppress it altogether. He has chosen rather
to recognize the dignity of man's moral nature, and, after
God's order, to make the moral stand out boldly, as best befits
a religious design, and especially a paraphrase of sacred story.

The notes have been added by the advice of a veteran critic.
Where controversial they have been submitted to the parties
interested.

In appending a chronological index of the pieces, the
author has only done what he wishes all the poets had done for
him. He has done it also in the hope that other writers, whom
the world will care more about, may one day do the same.

Thus these pieces are once more sent forth, with the prayer
that they may be not wholly without a mission in helping to
make a better and a happier world.

G. L. T.

541 HERKIMER STREET, BROOKLYN,
      June 25, 1885.

CONTENTS.

PROEM.

"Non Nobis, Domine."

"Not unto us, O Lord, not unto us, but unto thy name give glory."—Psalm 115 : 1.

I.

Not unto us, O Lord, not unto us
  The praise or honor, power, or glory be !
Our naked spirits bow in shame and dust,
  And offer only nothingness to thee.

II.

Not unto us !   How vain is mortal might,
  Our toils or talents, gifts, or growth or grace ;
Nothing and less than nothing in thy sight,
  Our works—ourselves !   Before thy glorious face,

III.

We blush t' appear, though prostrate. These poor straws,
  What are they 'mid thy infinite harvests white !
What are these dreams, to thy self-luminous laws !
  These drops of darkness, 'mid thy wonders bright !

IV.

Thou spheral sea of universal light !
   All else is born, and floats, and dies in thee ;
Thy being knows no limit and no night ;
   Thou wast, and art, and shalt forever be !

V.

Thy all-informing Spirit breathes and lives
   Through all thy works—thy bright perfections shown !
No power exists but thy volition gives,
   No work of good that is not all thine own.

VI.

Thy boundless, blest diffusion all things fills,
   Warms, quickens, kindles, actuates, inspires ;
Through being's soul thy sovereign soul distils ;
   Through all things flash, unspent, thy fruitful fires !

VII.

" Not unto us ;" the grass, the flowers, the trees
   Breathe in low whispers where the sunshine rains ;
" Not unto us ;" beast, bird, and brook, and breeze
   Responsive murmur o'er fields, woods, and plains.

VIII.

" Not unto us ;" with kneeling waves the sea
   Proclaims in reverence 'round a thousand shores ;
" Not unto us ;" throughout infinity,
   From space to space the star-voiced anthem pours.

IX.

" Not unto us ;" thy feeblest offspring sigh,
　　The animated motes through nature sown ;
" Not unto us ; " thy grandest creatures cry,
　　That burn with formless flames before thy throne.

X.

" Not unto us !"　How sweet to join the strain,
　　In self deliverance blissful and complete ;
And all our toils, successes, failures, pain,
　　To lose, O Christ Creator, at thy feet !

XI.

" Not unto us !"　Our humble gifts we bring,
　　Because thou askest all, and wilt receive :
O grant a nobler power to toil and sing,
　　To use one talent, and for more believe.

XII.

" Not unto us !"　O Lord of worlds supreme,
　　What good we work thou workest ; thine the praise !
O cleanse !　Light all our deeps with Truth's white beam !
　　And work in us, through us, to endless days !

ELIJAH THE REFORMER.

A BALLAD-EPIC.

----•-•----

I.

O SPIRIT from whose fiery breath all hero-souls are born,
Whose wondrous line of seers divine went forth the world to
    warn,
Teach me the strains to sing thy power in one of loftiest fame,
Whose godlike soul, while ages roll, still sets men's hearts
    aflame !
Teach me Elijah's spirit, rapt, Elijah's faith to sing,
Till snatched from time in flight sublime, his ardent soul
    takes wing ;
God's great REFORMER, greatest born, the type of all who burn
With heaven-sent fire to lift man higher ; O might his like
    return !
Then, then should our weak, doubting age learn faith in God
    again,
And heroes rise on longing eyes, to lead the race of men.

II.

The city by King Omri built stood on her far-famed hill,
With silver bought for talents twain, and named for Shemer[1]
    still ;
For Shemer, who there taught his corn and wine their amber
    glow,
Before her stately turrets rose, renowned so long ago,
Samaria, then queen of that revolted Israel
Whom Nebat's son, 'gainst Judah's line first tempted to rebel.
So fair, so grand that city shone, a mountain, splendor-crowned,
An opal in an emerald plain of vineyards sweeping 'round ;
Beyond the plain the circling range of Ephraim, bold and
    free,
Sank westward where soft Sharon dreams beside the bound-
    less sea.
Not Salem's self, on Zion throned, such matchless site could
    boast,
Nor one of thousand cities famed in all the ages lost.

III.

Now princely Ahab, Omri's son, possessed his father's
    throne,
And o'er ten tribes of Jacob's seed reigned sov'reign and
    alone.
From snow-crowned Hermon's towering range his sceptre
    swayed supreme,
To Judah's vine-impurpled dells, and Jordan's winding gleam ;

I. Kings 16 : 24.

From far-off Bashan's oak-clad hills, and Gilead, breathing
   balm,
To where majestic Carmel nods o'er ocean's sunset calm.
A goodlier realm of mount and plain and vale and lake and
   shore,
The sun ne'er saw, whose quenchless beams earth's thousand
   lands explore.
Nor slack was royal Ahab's hand, content with nature's toil,
Perennial streams, and grains and fruits that owned the gen-
   erous soil,
For arms and arts beneath his care in power and culture rose,
The triumphs of a land in peace, the terror of her foes.
Damascus twice, with Syria's kings in chivalry allied,
Beneath his arm, at God's command, bowed low her broken
   pride ;
Samaria's walls more grandly towered ; fair Jezreel smiled
   below ;
And from eight centuries night and curse woke dateless
   Jericho.[1]
O Shomeron,[2] had Salem's Lord, Jehovah, been alone
Thy trust, how might thy name have thrilled the ages, like
   her own !

IV.

   But ah ! from one deliberate crime, what sumless woes
   begin !
Since Nebat's impious son first dared—immortal in his sin !—

[1] I. Kings 16 : 34.
[2] Ibid. 16 : 24, Hebrew name in margin.

'Neath bestial forms of gold [1] th' Unknown, the Infinite to
    express,
How swift, how fearful Israel's lapse, how deep, how fathomless !
Six blood-red reigns in sixty years had marked that wrathful
    time,
Till Ahab rose o'er all before, in infamy sublime,
And he beneath whose godless thrift a mammon age had grown,
In pride portentous strove to drive Jehovah from his throne.
For Ahab's chosen bride and queen,[2] of Zidon's royal line,
Adored not Israel's God, but bowed at Baal's hostile shrine ;
That power [3] renowned from Libya's coast to Ormus' orient
    strand,
Phœnicia hoar, Pelasgic Greece, and every Punic land.
Osiris, Ammon, Belus, Bel, by Nile or Phrat he throve,
By some Hesperian Saturn owned, by some Olympian Jove ;
But Jove, with Rome's Panthéon, bowed before his conquer-
    ing shrine,
When Baal's priest was Rome's base lord,[4] and shamed her
    Cæsars' line.

[1] I. Kings 12 : 28, 29.
[2] Ibid. 16 : 30, 31.
[3] See McClintock and Strong's Biblical, Theological, and Ecclesiastical
Cyclopædia, articles on Baal, Baalim, Asherah, Ashtoreth, etc.
[4] Namely, when Heliogabálus, who had been consecrated a priest of the
Syrian sun-god Elagabálus (who was the same as the Phœnician Baal), became emperor of Rome, A.D. 219.   He exalted Baal above all the Greek
and Roman gods, proclaiming them to be only his servants, while he himself publicly officiated as Baal's priest, until his profligacy, which shamed
even fallen Rome, caused his assassination, by which Rome was delivered
from a monster, although he was then only eighteen years old.

E'en far-off Britain's Druid piles and cromlechs[1] tell his
    fame,
And Scotia's shapeless crumbling cairns still bear his mystic
    name.
Him Ahab's queen from Tyrian fanes to high Samaria bore,
With her, as Aprodítè[2] known on the loose Cyprian shore,
Foul Ashtoreth, the moon, or star, Astártè, heaven's lewd
    queen,
Ashérah, one, the same, adored with nameless rites obscene.

V.

Then on Samaria's beetling height, her steep Acropolis,
Idolatry's first temple[3] rose, its dark metropolis.
Solemn and vast the wonder loomed, a marble peristyle,
Whose ruins mocked the years, rebuilt in many a later pile.
There Baal's giant stature towered, with man-like form and
    face,
But brow and horns that spake the lord of all the belluine
    race ;

[1] "Traces of the idolatry symbolized under it [Baalism] are even found in
the British Isles, Baal, Bal, or Beal being, according to many, the name of
the principal Deity of the ancient Irish ; and on the tops of many hills in
Scotland there are heaps of stones called by the common people 'Bel's
Cairns,' where it is supposed that sacrifices were offered in early times."—
Statistical Account of Scotland, iii., 105 ; xi., 621.

[2] Ashtoreth or Asherah was the Syrian Venus, known as Aphroditè in profligate Cyprus and other Greek countries, the goddess of carnal love.

[3] I. Kings 16 : 32, 33. Profane authors mention the size and strength of
this famous temple, although perhaps they confound it with the one on Mount
Gerizim, which was afterward, under Antiochus Epiphanes, converted into
a temple of Jupiter Hellenius.—*Josephus, Antiq.* xii., v., 5.

Strength, rule, the generative powers terrestrial, blent in one,
With brute-like force, and human mind, and symbolled by
  the sun.[1]
And lewd Astártè's lustful groves on every hill were seen,
Where mysteries abhorred were taught beneath the shimmer-
  ing green,
Where priestesses of shame, like those of famed Mylitta's[2]
  dome,
Whose guilt sunk mighty Babylon, made God's pure land
  their home.
Oh, rueful day ! when Israel's king, with vain ambition wild,
For state-craft sold his God, and wooed Ethbaal's heathen
  child !
To bind his league with alien powers both faith and con-
  science sold,
And brought the harlot Jezebel, a tigress, to God's fold !
Around her board eight hundred priests of Baal, and the
  groves
Of vile Ashérah, riot loud, and boast their impious loves,
While Israel's altars fall, profaned, her priests to exile driven ;
Her warriors cowed, her matrons shamed, her maids to out-
  rage given ;
Till court and cot, debased alike, Jehovah's law blaspheme ;
And Virtue faints, dissolved and lulled in deep, luxurious
  dream.

---

[1] See Cyclopædia articles on Baal and Baalism.
[2] Mylitta, the Babylonian Venus, whose worship was one of the most
profligate known to antiquity.

PART SECOND. FROM GILEAD TO CARMEL.

I.

Then, like the cloudless thunder-bolt that cleaves the sum-
  mer sky,
Or like the whirlwind's burst that whelms the fleets that
  windless lie,
From unknown Tishbè's hamlet rude, in Gilead's wilds afar,
God's doom on that apostate land fell like a blazing star.
The Tishbite dread, ELIJAH, stands in Ahab's ivory hall !
His cloak the skin of mountain goat, his robe a mohair
  pall ;
His garb around his sinewy loins a rawhide belt confined ;
His hair and beard, like raven plumes, streamed dark along
  the wind.
A strong acacia's spiky stem, scarce smoothed, was in his
  hand ;
His feet were fleshless, callous, bare, and tawny as the sand ;
His brow, a beetling crag, o'erhung his swart and shaggy
  chest,
And 'neath its shades his eyes glanced keen as eagles' from
  their nest.
Remote from courts, corruption, crime, in that high, shepherd
  land,
With God alone his soul had grown to stature bold and
  grand ;

From Jacob's seed, or Jokshan's stock, unknown,[1] he stands
    God's seer ;
The Highlander of prophecy, God's glorious mountaineer ;
For many a wild, in many a land, and many a peak sublime,
Can tell how solitude with God breeds souls that conquer
    time.
  Such he who in that wondrous hall, unbidden, awed earth's
    state,
Till one man's upright majesty dwarfed all that kings call
    great.
That roof, of India's tusk inwrought, and Afric's mighty
    spoils,
Bestarred with rainbow gems, in zones of Ophir's fretted toils;
That dome's cerulean firmament, with zodiac fires o'erspread ;
That tessell'cd pave, whose storied sheen flung back the hues
    o'erhead ;
That regal throne, sublimely raised amid the mimic spheres,
Fade all, like glittering dreams, what time that awful form
    appears !
With right hand lifted to the winds, in act to bind the storm,
And eyes before whose steadfast gaze back cowered that scep-
    tred worm,
Like the dread sound from Ocean's deeps, when earthquakes
    jar his caves,

---

[1] There is much ground in the general character and conduct of Elijah to
suggest that he was not a Hebrew, but of some of the other numerous tribes
of Abrahamides settled on the Eastern frontier of Palestine. See Cyclopædia
articles on " Jokshan," etc.; also the views of several recent Oriental travellers
and scholars. He was, at all events, a typical Shemite seer.

The message came, or like the moan of spirits o'er the
waves !—
"As lives Jehovah, Israel's God, before whose face I
stand,
Nor summer's dew, nor winter's rain, shall slake this
guilty land
These months and years to come, except according to my
word
From God !"— He ceased.   Aghast they stood, nor king nor
menial stirred,
Palsied alike ! Unchallenged forth through court and gate he
passed,
From throngs who watched that day's light fade as though it
were earth's last.

II.

Woe to the land where Virtue dies, and Passion reigns
alone !
Where Lust, sublimed and deified, usurps Religion's throne !
Where flesh and blood, mere kneaded dust, in hot ferment
conspire,
Cloud Reason's sight, and Heaven's pure light, and set men's
souls on fire !
Woe to the age whose seers and bards, instinct with earth-
born flame,
Pervert divine philosophy to plead for swinish shame ;
And bow the awful gift of song, Heaven's highest chrism of
fire,

Changed to a foul and reeking slave, to serve accurst Desire !

Woe to the age when gold is god, and law a solemn jest

That helps the boldly vile to crush the noblest and the best !

When Mammon o'er cheap millions flings his gilded harness strong,

And drives them, tame beneath his lash, down broad highways of wrong,

While Truth's shrill clarion down the sky peals faintly o'er the rout,

And dust and fumes of earth and sin shut heaven's last sunlight out :

Then look for lightning ! God's red bolts must cleave the stifling gloom,

In love or wrath, to purge the world, or whelm in Sodom's doom.

III.

Rain ! Rain ! No rain ! No morning dew to bend the pleading flowers ;

No moisture dripping cool at dawn among the vine-clad bowers.

The empty clouds, with mocking pomp, on light vain winds float by,

And melt from sight at morn and even, in one unchanging sky.

The noontide beats, a billowy sea of fierce, relentless rays,

And morn and even's suns glow red, in sullen fiery blaze !

The fields are parched, the harvests scorched, the pastures
  brown and sere ;
The roaming, restless, wistful herds low hollow on the
  ear ;
The noisy rills are dry, the brooks creep from dead pools to
  pools,
Beneath whose banks the crowded fry scarce hide their finny
  schools ;
The buzzing tribes annoy the air with angry hum and sting ;
The panting fowls hide close, and fear the falcon's hovering
  wing ;
The gasping birds forget their songs and droop in cheerless
  shade ;
The grasshopper, and locust, dread, like fire the world invade ;
The ground is fevered, chapped, and baked; with dust the
  travellers choke ;
Sparks light the meads, the forests flame, the swamps and
  marshes smoke :
No more the fig-tree blossoms fair, no fruit is in the vine ;
The centuried olive's labor fails, the corn-fields droop and
  pine ;
The flocks, cut off, leave empty folds, that need no shepherd's
  care ;
The herds are perished from the stalls, devoured, consumed,
  and bare !
Famine ! Dire Famine, gaunt and grim, stalks o'er the guilty
  land !
And stark Starvation leads behind a glowering, ghastly band

Of woes and scourges, sorrows, crimes, shames, miseries untold,
That bow, and blast, and grind men's souls, with agony grown
  old !

IV.

Three years, three direful, nameless years, since heaven's
  great azure eye
Has dropped one pitying tear on man, from that remorseless
  sky !
And still the burning days roll on, and torturing months drift
  past,
Each fiercer in its fiery stress, more fearful than the last !
But where is he, that vengeful seer, whose word like lightning
  fell
On king and court,—enchained and dumb 'neath that un-
  earthly spell ?
From realm to realm the stern demand has vainly sought its
  prey,
While lulled by Cherith's rippling wave secure the hermit
  lay.
At morn and even, a strange long year, by heaven's deep mandate taught,
On noiseless wing his bread and meat the conscious ravens
  brought ;
Before his grot the torrent's wave his daily thirst sup-
  plied,
And God's great lore rapt more and more his soul from all
  beside.

One year alone with God, the Infinite ! Ah, who can tell
How high, how vast, the human soul such fellowship may
    swell !
How earth sinks down, how heaven's calm orb the soaring
    mind inspheres,
Space, time, form, motion, substance, self, all lost'when God
    appears !   .
But seraphs quit, to toil for man, the throne's unuttered
    glow,
And God himself, incarnate, stooped to die for mortal woe ,
And so, from raptest heights sublime, from ecstasies unknown,
Devotion's wing must earthward bend at sorrow's humblest
    moan.

V.

No rain ! E'en Cherith's bed ran dry ! Then far in Zidon's
    land
Sarepta's gate the prophet saw, a pilgrim, staff in hand.
The famished widow heard his plaint, Faith triumphed o'er her
    fears,
She gave her all, and lo, the store fed all, for months and
    years !
But there, 'mid that long miracle, while haggard Famine fled,
Dire sickness smote her one proud boy ; her only boy lay
    dead :   .
Then, anguish-wrung, " O Man of God," she cried, with grief
    undone,
" Why hast thou brought my sin to mind ! Why hast thou slain
    my son !"

Ah, who can tell how tenderness sleeps 'neath the sternest face,
And adamantine heroes catch from tears their noblest grace.
So he, whose look awed Ahab's throne, now clasps that cold
      dead child,
And flies to God with human cry, sharp, passionate, and wild.
" O God, why hast thou evil brought !   O God, send back this
      soul !"
And thrice he grasped that lifeless form, till Faith, through
      Death's control,
Burst its strong way, and chased on wing that spirit in its
      flight
Through worlds unknown, till 'neath God's throne it claimed
      him as its right,
And God said, " Go, return !"   Then life leapt through that
      frozen blood,
And Love cried : " Lo, by this I know thou art a seer of
      God !"

VI.

No rain ! No dew ! The last streams fail. The fields are
      dust and sand ;
No bread remains, and ghastly fear hangs dim o'er all the
      land.
Then royal Ahab rose to save his matchless steeds of state,
And passed with Obadiah forth from high Samaria's gate.
" Go through the land, search all the springs, perchance some
      grass remains
In mountain dells, or marge of lakes, or Jordan's flooded
      plains."

Each fared his way, the search was vain : then God bespake
    his seer :
"Go meet proud Ahab, fear him not, my time for rain draws
    near."
  Then came the word, " Elijah calls !" In haste the monarch
    turned,
While long-nursed hate and mad revenge within him fiercely
    burned :
"Is't thou, thou troubler of this land?" in instant rage he
    cries ;
" Not *I*, but *thou*, art Israel's curse !" that iron lip replies ;
" Because Jehovah's law ye scorn, in Baal to delight !
Go bring all Israel now to me, on Carmel's hallowed height ;
Bring Baal's seers, four hundred men and fifty, bring them
    all,
And those four hundred more who feast in Jezebel's lewd
    hall !"
The monarch heard ; on Carmel's crown now swarms a count-
    less throng,
With one brave soul to stand for God 'gainst myriads in the
    wrong.
On Carmel's crown, that far o'erlooks Esdraelon's mighty
    plain,
Whence ancient Kishon's gathered streams roll westward to
    the main.
There Barak's [1] host, at Deborah's word, on Sisera's chariots
    fell,

---

[1] Judges, chapters 4 and 5.

And Kishon rose to whelm God's foes with sudden, wrathful
    swell.

There Gideon's band from Canaan's land the fierce invader
    swept,

And there fell Saul and Jonathan, while Israel's daughters wept.

There good Josiah [1] rashly fought, and fell, when Egypt's lord,

Inspired, though Gentile, prophesied Jehovah's warning
    word.

There, age on age, millenniums through, have realms been
    lost and won,

There Gog and Magog [2] fall at last, before God's Conquering
    Son.

But not till earth's last conflict joins Esdraelon shall behold

A grander day than that which dawned on Carmel's top of
    old,

When God's great prophet dared a realm, its priests and
    king defied,

And stood alone for God and right, no mortal on his side !

VII.

Then through that throng, with heart on fire, he preached
    Jehovah's law,

To rouse their hearts to patriot glow, or thrill with heavenly
    awe ;

" How long thus halt, ignobly dumb ! nor own your Maker's
    claim !

[1] II. Chron. 35 : 20-24.
[2] Rev. 20 : 8, 9, and 16 : 16, and poem " Armageddon," p. 202.

If he be God, serve him ! If not, then bow to Baal's shame !"
  No answering word ! Not one ? O God, can truth be sunk
    so low,
That not a nation's challenged host one champion can show ?
O sight to make brave angels blush, and stir th' Eternal ire,
When conscious millions, coward souls, tread manhood in the
    mire,
Choke conscience down, and stifle shame, and 'neath the sun's
    broad smile,
Stand basely weak, flout heaven, and dare—dare only to be
    vile !
Then spake that dauntless soul : " I stand alone God's prophet
    here,
But Baal boasts four hundred men, elate with royal cheer ;
Let them therefore bring bullocks twain, and choose and slay
    their own,
And on a fireless altar pile, invoking Baal alone,
Your Sun-god strong, whose realm is fire, whose crown is
    dazzling rays,
Let him, in his own realm defied, defend his crown, and
    blaze !
But I'll invoke Jehovah's name, and he whose flame replies,
Let him be God !"—The nation hears, and answering plaudits
    rise.
  Evasion past, the steers are brought, and Baal's offering
    slain :
From early morn till glowing noon his followers howl in
    vain :

Fierce, frantic, wild, they beat the ground, and gash their
 reeking sides,
While biting sarcasm does its work, and righteous scorn
 derides.
" Cry out ! Bawl [1] loud ! He's sure a god ! Perchance brown
 study sways
His absent thoughts ; or nature's call, like mortals, he obeys ; [2]
Perchance he journeys ! Nay, perchance he takes his nap at
 noon ;
Bawl louder ! Split his stupid ears ! You'll surely rouse him
 soon !"
They leap, they bound, they wheel and spin, in furious frenzy
 whirled—
The mad, demoniac Dervish-dance of all the Orient world !
The dream that puts mere flesh for faith, mere muscle puts
 for mind,
Excitement puts for God, and leads unreasoning millions
 blind.
Ah, dark Fanaticism ! still in every age the same,
For thee, through all time's years, ne'er yet from heaven one
 answer came.
Strange imps alone, and goblins weird, flock gibbering at thy
 cry,
When God binds these, not hell itself can mutter one reply.

---

[1] Bawl, the literal rendering of the Hebrew.
[2] See Whedon, *in loc.*, and R. V. A just sarcasm on the heathen religions. Jud. 3 : 24.

VIII.

Then, while the sunset hour sped on, in accents bold and
　　clear,
Elijah bade th' attesting tribes to mark *his* deed draw near.
God's ancient altar, far-renowned in centuries of yore,
A shapeless, moss-grown heap, he rears with pious care once
　　more,
And twelve fresh stones he adds, each tribe presenting thus
　　anew
To plead with God that changeless vow to Abraham's offspring
　　due.
The victim bleeds, the pile is scanned by strict and hostile
　　eyes ;
Then, in the gaze of thousand foes, aloud once more he cries,
" From yon perennial fountain pour four barrels on the shrine,
Once, twice, and thrice !" 'Tis done.   On stole the sacred
　　hour divine,
The hour of evening sacrifice, when God, of old attent,
Had heard well-pleased man's voice in prayer, and many an
　　answer sent.
　　Then forth he stood, that one weird man, before dark Ahab's
　　throne,
While Baal's seers glanced vengeance fell, and called on God
　　alone.
O'er ocean's boundless breast, afar, warm tides of splendor
　　rolled,
Where the great sun, his day's course done, swam down a sea
　　of gold ;

And woods, and slopes, and bosky dells, in heaven's own
    brightness glowed,

All nature, crowned, stood reverent 'round, to hail her con-
    quering God.

Sublime, serene, that lone form looms, embathed in sunset
    now,

And more than mortal majesty is gleaming on his brow :

He prays : his few calm, clarion tones on night's faint
    zephyrs swell :

" JEHOVAH, GOD OF ABRAHAM, OF ISAAC, ISRAEL,

LET IT BE KNOWN THIS DAY THAT THOU IN ISRAEL ART LORD,

AND I, THY SERVANT, ALL THESE THINGS HAVE DONE BUT AT
    THY WORD !"

IIe ceased.   See ! see !   A ruddier flash o'erspreads the pomp
    on high !

An awful cloud of beamy fire sweeps eddying down the sky !

And from its sparkling bosom fall broad sheets of blinding
    flame,

While thunders shock the trembling world, and peal Jehovah's
    name !

The fiery whirlpool falls !   In flame consumed th' oblation
    flies !

And water, dust, and calcined stones, have vanished from their
    eyes !

The trench alone, with cinders strewn, remains to mark the
    pyre,

Where God most High, at a mortal's cry, answered from
    heaven by fire !

Then, from a prostrate nation, rose the long and loud
　　acclaim,
" THE LORD IS GOD !　THE LORD IS GOD !　JEHOVAH IS HIS
　　NAME !"
From rank to rank, through camps and tribes, the shout rang
　　glad and free,
Like trumpets echoing through the hills, or thunders of the
　　sea !
" THE LORD IS GOD !　THE LORD IS GOD !"　The clouds roll back
　　the sound,
And airy tongues, from height to height, the answering shout
　　rebound.
　　Then rose that fateful voice once more : " Take Baal's
　　prophets, all !
Let none escape !" A nation, roused, obeys the righteous
　　call ;
And Kishon's ancient stream, that erst whelmed Jabin's proud
　　array,
With impious gore ran red once more, on God's great reckon-
　　ing day.
And still the wandering Arab points where fell Jehovah's
　　flame,
And bows with awe, where kings have stood and trembled at
　　that name :
The hollow burned in Carmel's crest, the rock by Kishon's
　　flood,
Jehovah's changeless witnesses, his seals of fire and blood.

IX.

Lo, now, where Carmel's topmost dome o'erlooks the western deep,
Two shadowy forms, while daylight fades, their high, lone
vigil keep.
One prostrate travails, bowed to dust, by prayer's strong
anguish pressed,
And one stands tall against the sky, and scans the darkening
west.
Lo, God's great prophet prays for rain! A mortal and a
.   worm
Wrestles with Him who guides the winds, whose chariot is the
storm!
Wrestles with that resistless might all-conquering faith sup-
plies,
Till God cries "Hold! Thou hast thy wish!" That answer
thrilled the skies!
O'er ocean's waste the wandering mists a strange compulsion
owned,
The freshening night-breeze moister blew, more deep the surf
wail moaned;
"Go look again, seven times!" The seventh a dull and
brassy band
Along the far horizon grew, and, like a human hand,
One speck of cloud rose slow, and spread along the laboring
air,
That breathless hung, or quivering owned the tempest gathering there.

"Up! Fly to Ahab! Bid him yoke, and speed his chariot
down,
Nor halt for rain through all the plain, till safe in Jezreel's
town !"
E'en while he mounts the clouds grow black, they toil, and
writhe and roll,
In angry majesty of gloom, like night, from pole to pole !
Winds rend the mountain ! Thunders boom ! Forked lightnings crash around !
Great pattering drops fall fast ! A hush ! A rising, rushing
sound,
And then, with smoke, and surge, and roar, the great rain
smites the ground.
The windy deluge howls and raves, but through its blinding
wrack
God's servant feels Jehovah's hand, like whirlwinds, at his
back ;
And, girt, before the bounding steeds, on tireless foot he
springs,
Nor halts, till, late, at Jezreel's gate he lights, fresh as from
wings !

X.

O rain ! Sweet rain ! Baptismal rain ! When Nature's pulse
grows faint,
When, fever-blasted, earth expires, or gasps her voiceless
plaint,
Then welcome, summer's mighty rain ! Pour, heaven's best
blessing, pour !

Leap, keen wild lightnings, through the gloom! Glad thunders shout and roar!

Pour on! surge on! ye sky-born floods! Drink, Earth, O drink
thy fill!

Up! clap your hands, ye streams new-born, and laugh from
every hill!

Lift your great arms, ye mighty groves! Fling out your
bannered leaves!

And bend your tops in billowy joy, as the blue ocean heaves!

Wake from the dust, ye perished flowers, put on your bright
array!

Burst into green, ye thankful fields! Birds, tune your gladdest
lay!

Skip o'er the hills, ye blithesome flocks! Herds, gambol on the
plain!

Go forth, O man, and bless thy God, who gives the summer rain!

PART THIRD. FROM CARMEL TO SINAI.

I.

Ah, Earth can cool her fiery rage, when heaven's sweet
showers descend,

And godless man, e'en from a throne, before God's voice can
bend;

But O, what power shall tame the mad, unreasoning, frantic tide

Of woman's passion, vanity, ambition, foiled, defied!

"So do my gods to me, and more, before to-morrow's shade,

If like the life of those, my seers, *thy* life I have not made!"

So raved the Tyrian sorceress, unawed by God's own hand,
While he whose word the lightnings heard fled, trembling,
from the land !
From Jezreel fair, through Issachar, Manasseh, Ephraim wide,
Through Benjamin his swift course sped, and Judah, Israel's
pride,
Till far beyond Beersheba's wells, the green world's southern
bound,
Alone he trod the sandy waste, the desert's dread profound.

II.

The Desert ! Earth herself, at last, a ruin dark and wild,
A mother with an iron breast, and brow that never smiled;
That never down her stony face has dropped one tender tear;
Vastness and silence ! solitude sublime, and stern, and drear !
But ah, from man's apostate shame, how welcome Nature's
frown !
Refuge for hunted souls more sweet than grandeur's lap of
down ;
Nurse of strong spirits, school where God forever felt and
nigh,
Bids mortals rise and walk the skies, and breathe eternity.

III.

On, on along the trackless waste, through all that burning
day,
The exile marched, with none but God to guide his lonely
way ;

At sunset, 'neath a stunted shrub his fainting frame he cast,
And cried," Great God, so near me now, let this day be my last !
I am not better than my sires, before thy foes who fell ;
Lo, 'tis enough ! I long in peace, with them and thee, to
    dwell !"
Thus he who dares a realm in arms, whose eagle faith brings
    down
Fires, lightnings, whirlwinds at his word, on Carmel's awful
    crown,—
Whose thews of steel with Ahab's wheel for four long leagues
    keep pace
As on he speeds his foaming steeds through all that headlong
    race,—
In mortal weakness faints at last, when all the strife is o'er ;—
What marvel heroes falter once, where millions falter more !
Then heaven's best, sweetest benison, for God's beloved kept,
Stole soft o'er every languid sense, and, bathed in balm, he
    slept.
" Rise, eat !" Beside the blossoming broom [1] a mild-eyed angel
    stands !
A cake on coals,[1] a cooling draught, are near him on the sands :
He eats and sleeps. Once more that voice : " Thy journey is
    too long,
God feeds and guides the souls he loves. Rise, eat and drink,
    be strong !"
Then forty days and forty nights, unhungering and untired,

---

[1] See McClintock and Strong's Cyc., Article " Juniper."

Through Paran's boundless solitudes he moved, with strength
    inspired,
Till Horeb's giant form, afar, rose shadowy on his sight,
And now he trod the mount of God, on Sinai's awful height.
  O mount of God, earth's grandest mount, thy hoary peaks
    sublime,
Jehovah's witnesses, still speak his praise through earth and
    time !
On thee the law that lights the world, 'mid light from heaven
    was given,
And God's great name he wrote in flame on marbles thunder-
    riven !
Oh, meet thy lone and silent crags, for him who strove once
    more
To bring back man to heaven's pure plan revealed on thee of
    yore !
Aye, meet the great Restorer stand where the Lawgiver stood
Six hundred years before, and so talk face to face with God !

IV.

  "What doest thou here, Elijah ?" Hark ! that voice, like
    organ's swell,
Calm, deep, divine, æolian-toned, these rocks remember well.
Through vales and dells and chasms and caves the breeze-like
    murmurs roll:
Then in his cavern, reverent bowed, replies that listening soul:
" Lord God of hosts, for thy great name my zeal like fire has
    burned,

For Israel's seed have scorned thy law, thy holy altars spurned;

Thy priests are fled ; thy seers are slain ; one only breathes,
and he,

Hunted for life, from rage and strife, flees, trembling, Lord,
to thee !"

"Go forth and stand upon the mount, before the Lord."
He went,

While God passed by.   A mighty wind the rock-ribbed mountain rent ;

Before that black tornado's stream the rent rocks whirl and
crash,

Till splintered granite flies like boughs when lightning rends
the ash !

But God was not in all the storm.   Then woke an earthquake's
shock ;

Plains roll in waves, hills skip like lambs, the globe's foundations rock ;

Crags torn from crags down gulfs unknown dash thundering
through the gloom,

Earth, shuddering, groans and reels and moans, and dreads
her latest doom.

God was not there.   The murky air flashed forth in omens dire,

And lambent flames dart dazzling 'round, and wrap the mount
in fire ;

From cliff to cliff, from peak to peak, pale ghostly lightning
plays ;

The rocks explode !   On Alpine spires an hundred beacons
blaze !

An hundred white St. Elmos dance on every gleaming height !
An hundred weird auroras arch the mount with wizard light !
But God was not in wind, nor flame, nor earthquake's Titan
　　jar,
They only flew before his march, glad heralds of his car :
A hush profound.　Then, like the thrill of night-winds through
　　the pine,
Once more that still, small voice swelled clear, harmoniously
　　divine.
　Then rose the seer, with mantled head, and heard, with
　　reverent awe,
" What doest thou here, Elijah ?　Go, avenge my outraged law.
Make crafty Házael, Syria's king, in fair Damascus' gate,
And fiery Jehu, Nimshi's son, anoint o'er Israel's state ;
Then speed where Shaphat's pious heir ploughs Abel's deep-
　　tilled soil
With twelve strong yokes, and on him pour the olive's hal-
　　lowing oil,
Seer in thy stead, — a threefold doom !　Who 'scapes the
　　Syrian's sword
Shall Jehu slay ; who flees from him dies at Elisha's word !
Yet know thou well that not alone thou standest true to me ;
Seven thousand loyal souls remain, who ne'er have bowed
　　the knee
At Baal's foul, ignoble shrine, nor kissed his form profane ;
Take heart, faith lives, and from the dust my truth shall rise
　　and reign."

PART FOURTH. FROM SINAI TO NEBO.

I.

SLOW years roll on. Wars come and go. Samaria's guilty towers
Are saved by God, whose arm, belied, smites Syria's banded powers.
Peace comes once more, and field and town alike her empire bless,
And cities build, and vineyards bloom with thrift and plenteousness.
And none more fair than Naboth's smiled, by Jezreel's sheltering wall,
Hard by where, bowered in groves divine, rose Ahab's Ivory Hall.
For broad domains and gardens fair Samaria's lord still sighs,
And oft on Naboth's vine-clad slopes he bends insatiate eyes.
But the bold yeoman claims with pride the freehold of his sires,
For in his sturdy, steadfast soul, glow freedom's native fires.
Then despot power and slavish fear must stain the earth once more,
And free-born Naboth, outraged, slain, lies weltering in his gore !
"Rise ! Seize thy wish !" the harpy cries; "that stubborn churl lies dead !"
Then forth to grasp the blood-stained field the perjured tyrant sped.

With eager eyes he scans the prize, he bursts the vineyard
  gate—
Then halts, aghast! Before him starts that awful form of
  fate!
" Hast found me, O mine enemy ?" in cowering fear he cries :
" I *have* found thee !" in tones of doom that dreaded voice
  replies.
" Because before Jehovah's sight thy manhood thou hast sold,
Thy sceptre, too, all crime and wrong to work for lust and
  gold,
Thus saith the Lord, all miseries dire shall haunt thy guilty
  life ;
Thy seed shall fail, thy manly race cut off in shame and
  strife ;
Thy house, like that of Nebat's son, in infamy shall stand,
A proverb of reproach, a curse and warning in this land !
Who dies of Ahab in the town devouring dogs shall tear ;
Who dies abroad shall feed, abhorred, the carrion birds of
  air !
Yea, Jezebel, by Jezreel's wall, the howling pack shall rend.
Till Naboth's blood, required by God, pursue thee to the
  end !"
The king, appalled, his purple rent, in terror, fear, and shame ;
The Tishbite dread unanswering sped, and vanished as he
  came.

II.

On roll the years of strife and sin. On works that withering
  doom !

'Neath Ramoth's towers the Syrian shaft sends Ahab to the
    tomb.

Vain his disguise, his treachery vain, God wings the doubtful
    dart,

As, vengeful, through the conscious air, it seeks th' apostate's
    heart.

Dogs lap his blood by Jezreel's pool, deaths chase his godless
    son,

Moab rebels, new perils rise, the kingdom is undone.

    Then, death-struck, on his couch of pain, cried Ahab's
      impious heir,

"Send swift to Ekron's god, and ask of Baal-Zebub, there,

If from this wound I yet shall live?" In haste th' embassage
    hies,

When, spectre-like, an unknown form confronts their startled
    eyes!

Aged, but unbent by years, he stood; a man of iron frame,

Broad-browed and bronzed, with port sublime, and eyes that
    smote like flame.

His shaggy robe, untanned, and black, was spoiled from
    mountain fold,

And down his breast his mighty beard, a silver cataract
    rolled.

A leathern case of parchment rolls across his bosom hung,

And at his side, in leathern scrip, his scanty rations swung.

A strong acacia's time-worn stem that owned the toils of years,

His left hand grasped; his right, upraised, proclaimed the
    prince of seers.

He asked not who, nor whence, nor why they sped, but like a
    knell
Whose midnight clang stuns with a pang, the fateful message
    fell.
" Is it because no God remains in Israel's land, accurst,
Ye seek a heathen shrine obscene, their vilest and their
    worst ?
The fly-god foul, at Ekron's shrine, Philistia's hostile boast ?
Is Shiloh fled ? Are patriots dead ? Are faith and shame
    both lost ?
Back to the king ye serve, and say, thus saith the Lord
    most high,
'Hope not to quit that couch of pain, but know that thou
    shalt die !
For Naboth's blood from Ahab's line shall ne'er be washed
    away,
Till kings shall learn the rights of man, and own Jehovah's
    sway !' "
Back through Samaria's lofty gates the awestruck courtiers
    fled ;
They told their tale ; the monarch raved, yet trembled, on his
    bed.
" 'Tis he ! 'Tis he ! our ancient foe, the Tishbite wild !" he cries ;
" Ho ! Guards ! Up ! Mount ! This day I swear that hoary
    rebel dies !"

III.

The gates fly wide. With clattering rout the fifty thunder
    past ;

O'er hill and plain sweeps on the train, till Carmel looms at
 last.
There, near his grot, and 'mid his schools, the prophet sits
 serene,
Where Carmel's side, o'er landscapes wide, uplifts its wall of
 green ;
Where sweeps the view o'er hills and groves, vineyards, and
 golden grain,
Eastward to Jordan's gorge profound, and westward to the
 main.
" Thou man of God, the king hath said come down !" in rough
 command
The captain shouts, with brandished sword that glitters in
 his hand.
" If such I am, let fire from heaven consume thee, and thy
 crew !"
The dread seer spake ; that voice of old th' obedient light-
 nings knew ;
One blinding flash, with instant crash, shakes heaven's blue
 calm profound,
And all that impious troop lie scorched and blackened on the
 ground !
Swift speeds the tale ; the next fierce band lies blasted with
 the first,
Till e'en dark Baal's votaries dread Jehovah's thunder-burst ;
But still that mad, unhumbled wretch, by sin's last fury driven,
Makes war with God, whose bolts, defied, his armaments have
 riven.

His rage obeyed, one fifty more in silent terror ride,

But halt far off ; their chief alone climbs Carmel's fire-scathed
　　side ;

'Mid ghastly forms of steed and man, in mangled disarray,

Still frowning godless hate in death, he takes his trembling
　　way ;

" O man of God, spare, spare these souls !" he cries, and pros-
　　trate falls,

O'erwhelmed with awe.　God's angel saw, and thus, unseen,
　　he calls :

" Rise, go down with him, fear him not, Jehovah guards thy
　　path !"

Then, calm and clear, the dauntless seer meets all an empire's
　　wrath :

The same dire words, nor more, nor less, he speaks ;—no
　　tongue replies ;

Fear palsies all.　He quits the hall ; the mad blasphemer
　　dies.

IV.

　Jehoram reigns.　Still Ahab's seed, by Naboth's blood pursued,

Shall prove that dire, relentless curse that haunts the mur-
　　derer's brood.

In Edom's vale, by Moab's bounds, Elisha's awful word

Brings stern rebuke for Ahab's sin, but rescue from the Lord.

For David's son the burning waste with cooling streams o'er-
　　flows,

And Israel's sword, in wrath divine, o'erwhelms her envious
　　foes.

False Syria's powers against God's land plot oft their dark
    campaign,
But one man's word, forewarned of God, makes all their
    onsets vain.
Samaria, saved, attests his power, whom fiery hosts attend ;
But glory flees from Ahab's line that nears its direful end.
  From Ramoth's towers, where Ahab fell, the smitten Joram
      flies ;
From Ramoth's towers, ordained by God, the fiery Jehu
    hies,
Anointed king by Heaven's command in Joram's forfeit place,
And called to wipe from earth the last of Ahab's guilty race.
By Naboth's field, with vengeful arm, he bends a mighty
    bow,
Whose lightning shaft unerring speeds, and lays th' apostate
    low.
In Naboth's plot, God's word fulfilled, th' insulted corse is cast,
And Jehu's wheels toward Jezreel's gates burn onward fierce
    and fast.
There Jezebel's still tameless pride with scorn the conqueror
    hailed,
Fierce Jezebel, before whose hate sublime Elijah quailed !
False Jezebel, whose ruthless craft not Naboth's life with-
    stood !
Foul Jezebel, whose baleful spell wrought woes, a boundless
    flood,
Whose whoredoms, witchcrafts, sorceries, had filled the land
    with blood !

From where her palace window high o'erhangs the gate's
    proud arch,
With shameless brow and spiteful tongue she taunts the
   . conqueror's march ;
Till, from her lofty casement flung, her battered, gory frame
Beneath th' avenger's heel is trod, then left to dogs and shame.
The howling pack, foretold of God, her mangled members
    rend ;
The proverb of her sex in pride, in infamy, and end !
And seventy heads of Ahab's sons, in ghastly heaps, next
    morn,
In retribution swift and stark, his ivory gates adorn ;
Till righteous Naboth's guiltless blood, in treacherous outrage
    shed,
Has hurled the last of Ahab's race to rot among the dead ;
Blotted from earth, with Baal's crew ! as chaff in whirlwinds
    driven,
By him who heard the Tishbite's word, and wrought the doom
    of heaven !
A doom that flames God's righteous wrath at wrongs, by
    small or great,
And thunders forth th' oppressor's curse, th' apostate's crime
    and fate !

V.

  O brave, strong souls, who toil with God in every land and
    age,
And keep the music of his march, 'mid earth's discordant
    rage,

Faint not, fail not, the hour shall come, when, life's last
    conflict won,
God's hero-souls shall taste, e'en here, th' eternal calm begun.
That hour drew nigh. God's seer approved, time's matchless
    son of faith,
Must win one deathless victory more, the victory over Death ;
Must 'scape the general doom of man, his goblin foe despised,
And leap triumphant into life, by faith immortalized.

  Oh, dread, glad whisper, dim, unknown, that taught one
    soul like mine,
In deep, clear, cloudless trust to hold that nameless dream
    divine,
That voice by mortal ear unheard, nor doubt, nor boast the
    power,
Calm, silent, still, to wait God's will, content till that grand
    hour !

VI.

  It dawns. Instinct, yet speechless still, he takes his last
    long way ;
But first to Shaphat's son, inspired — "At Gilgal halt, I
    pray ;
God calls to Bethel, there to bless the college of his seers."
"As lives Jehovah, lives thy soul, my guide these wondrous
    years,
I will not leave thee !" On they trod to Bethel's turrets
    hoar,
Where Jacob dreamed, and youths like him still pondered
    heaven's high lore.

Forth came the prophets, youth and sage, to greet their head
    renowned,
With reverent looks and conscious souls, touched deep with
    woe profound.
That form revered they scan once more, and hail, with sacred
    awe,
God's mighty champion, he whose word brought back Jeho-
    vah's law.
His charge they hear that law to guard, to heed its least
    command,
And brave a thousand deaths to drive dark Baal from the land.
Then brief farewells, earth's last for them, as whispering sad,
    they say :
" Know'st thou thy guide, e'en from thy side, God's voice shall
    call this day ?"
" Yea, yea, too well, too well I know ; forbear !" Elisha cries ;
Yet tears will start when true souls part, as life's long memo-
    ries rise.
" Heaven-sent I go to Jericho. I pray thee tarry here."
" As lives thy God I leave thee not !" still spake Meholah's
    seer.
Then on they urge their mystic march down Cherith's lonely
    vale,
While he who erst dwelt there with God recounts that won-
    drous tale.
Those towers, of old by God o'erthrown, rebuilt, now greet
    their gaze,
With palmy shade and grateful rest from noontide's fiery rays.

Again the schools around their head in mournful homage
    throng,
And on the stores his lips distill dwell lovingly and long.
Not Greece's bright isles, while Homer's song its deathless
    numbers poured,
Nor Attic groves on Plato's tongue, so lingered and adored.

VII.

Earth's last grand labor now is wrought, the schools are all
    reviewed
By him who knows the worth of lore, though reared in soli-
    tude ;
For grace and knowledge, hand in hand, fulfil Redemption's
    plan,
And he who rails at learning owns himself blind guide for
    man.
Fit work for time's sublimest seer, on life's sublimest verge,
To hold back heaven one glorious day, on mortal youth to
    urge
The toils that form and fire the soul, 'neath Truth's bright
    flag unfurled ;
That shape the coming age, and light the minds that light
    the world !
Too fast, too fast the sun rides on ; too long this fond delay
That chains to earth a soul on fire for heaven's empyreal
    day !
The hour has struck to turn from man, from mortal smile
    or frown,
And meet the state from heaven's own gate already marching
    down ;

Yet one tried friend shall view that end, and live to tell the
    sight
To cheer brave souls while onward rolls earth's endless war
    for Right.
The same meek quest, the same reply : " I speed to Jordan's
    ford,
I pray thee wait." "I leave thee not, so help me Israel's
    Lord !"
Elisha's faith thrice tried, thrice proved, no more God's will
    demands ;
On Jordan's brink the hero folds his mantle in his hands ;
He smites the waves ; th' obedient deeps roll back, with tune-
    ful roar,
Where Israel's host dry-shod had crossed, six centuries before,
And left the cairn beneath the waves,[1] to mark the path they trod,
Beheld to-day, while fared that way the wondrous seer of God !
Toward Moab's wilds, where Moses' dust was laid so long ago
By God's own hand, of men ne'er scanned, they walked, serene
    and slow.
Toward Nebo's top, whence Moses viewed God's land with
    raptured gaze,
Moves he who soon shall hail the noon of heaven's unclouded
    blaze.
They talked : "What shall I ask for thee, before I quit thy
    sight ;
The moments fly." Elisha then, "On me, in twofold might,
Thy spirit rest." "A hard request, yet if thine eyes shall see
What time I rise, then thine the prize. If not, it shall not be."

---

[1] See poem on " The Passage of Jordan," p. 89, stanza XIX.

VIII.

A light that burst the concave sky! A shock, like earthquake's sound!

A whirlwind tore the mountain hoar, and shook the steadfast
ground!

And wheels of fire and steeds of flame, by God's strong angels
driven,

Between those two tempestuous flew, and snatched God's seer
to heaven!

Up! Up! Amid the thunder's shout, the dreadless mortal
rode,

And flamed afar on dazzling car along his path to God!

His beard's white streamer floats in light, his mantle drifts
below,

Beneath his team the sunset clouds like smitten forge-fires
glow!

On jasper tire, by hoofs of fire, with lightning ardor hurled,

He sweeps on high, and spurns the sky, and quits th' astonished
world!

On wheels that blaze with bickering rays he mounts the road
sublime,

Where Enoch erst ascended first, amid the dawn of time!

Around his chariot, countless poured, heaven's harnessed
seraphim

With trump and lyre swell high and higher heaven's conquering hero-hymn.

O'er gulfs of space, ethereal fields, th' ecstatic anthems
roll,

While life transformed, celestial, thrills his raptured frame
    and soul !

Immortal life through mortal mould like harmless lightning
    ran,

And all was fire, that erst was flesh ; was mind, but yet was
    man !

On, on o'er plains and heights untrod, and calm cerulean
    deeps,

Near and more near heaven's steadfast sphere, th' harmonious
    convoy sweeps ;

Till domes diaphanous, divine, white piles of quarried light,

Swim wide before, loom vast, and soar, a city infinite !

A city built of crystal gold, with jasper walls surrounded ;

On jaspers, sapphires, emeralds, and sea-green beryls founded ;

Where chalcedony, sardonyx, and sardius are blending

Their cross-fires with the topaz's glow, with chrysolite con-
    tending ;

With chrysoprase, and amethyst, and jacinth's flash amazing ;

And gates that blush, one rosy pearl, with diamond frostwork
    blazing !

A city never needing sun, nor moon, nor candle's shining,

Whose light is God, whose golden day knows never night's
    declining !

That city throbs with generous joy to hail the seer immortal,

Who drives, as never mortal drove, on to its radiant portal !

Its airy gates, a diamond dream, on sapphire wheels unfold ;

The convoy's passed ; one glimpse, earth's last — palms !
    crowns ! and harps of gold !

PART FIFTH. FROM NEBO TO HERMON.

I.

Earth's last? Ah no! A thousand years sweep o'er this
    whirling ball ;
And nations grow, and empires sink, and races rise and fall.
God's Eden-promise, fresh through time, its bound ordained
    has run,
And now on earth Messiah stands, Incarnate God the Son.
Three years of miracle for man, of toil all worlds to cheer,
Are all fulfilled ; the end is nigh ; time's central hour draws near.
Then He by whom, in pangs unknown, earth's winepress must
    be trod,
'Neath soaring Hermon's [1] snow-capped dome, for strength
    cries out to God.
Lo, while he prays, what beams divine through all his vest-
    ments glow !
They gleam more bright than Hermon's crown of dread,
    eternal snow !
The sun-flash lightens from his face, confest as God ! and
    there
Two dazzling shapes, of mortal mould, walk with him on the air!
  'Tis he ! 'Tis he ! the hero-seer ! and he the law who gave !
With Him who sent them both, and now himself has stooped
    to save !
'Tis he who braved for God and right a realm's apostate ire,

---

[1] For Hermon, instead of Tabor, see Whedon, and other modern com-
mentaries.

Wrought deeds sublime, then leapt from time in God's own
    car of fire !

'Tis he! He lives! He reigns enthroned, and bears from
    worlds above

God's own omnipotence to gird Messiah's grief and love !

The seal of God for all his toil, his high, heroic worth,

He stands alone of all God's seers, with God revealed on
    earth.

'Tis he, who, born a mountaineer, the mountains loved for aye,

Whom Gilead, Carmel, Horeb knew, and Nebo, in life's day ;

And not from earth his feet can rest till there on Syria's
    height,

He stands, where Moses prayed to stand, in Shenir's [1] daz-
    zling light !

With Moses stands !—That last fond prayer,[2] delayed, but not
    denied,

Remembered fifteen centuries, no longer God can chide !

And now on Lebanon, conjoined, stand these two souls
    sublime,

Twin heroes of the elder world, grand master-souls of time !

II.

With him who *gave* the law stands he who wrought its
    great *reform*,

---

[1] *Shenir*, a *breastplate*, in allusion to its glittering ice-cap and glaciers, the
most ancient Amorite name of the mountain which the Phœnicians called Si-
rion, and the Hebrews, Hermon.

[2] Deut. 3 : 23–26.

And grandly did and dared for God, though life were one long
      storm.
His eagle spirit braved the blast, o'er grief and death soared
      higher,
Till now, amid the seraphim he stands, a soul of fire !
God's minister plenipotent, he serves the great I AM
Till earth, redeemed, shall hymn the song of Moses and the
      Lamb.
And now with Moses and the Lamb in fellowship divine,
They talk how death shall work out life, in God's supreme
      design.
Of earth's Redemption all their talk, the glory of the cross ;
The Love that dies to save a world from endless death and
      loss ;
Dies not by accidental wrong, mobbed, martyred without
      plan,
But dies as given in eldest heaven, before all worlds began.
And he who led one Exodus, the night of History's [1] birth,
Bowed there to Him who leads through time the Exodus of
      earth ;
And he who brought back Israel's tribes to own Jehovah's
      sway
Adored God's Son, whose sceptre mild all earth shall yet
      obey.
Then time shall end, and suns expire, but they who've kept
      God's word,

---

[1] Bunsen declares that " History was born on that night " of the exodus
from Egypt.

Through heaven's unending age shall dwell forever with the
    Lord.
Blest rest ! Elysium undefiled ! So ours that portion be,
How sweet to toil for God below, then—Immortality !

PART SIXTH. EPILOGUE.

I.

O seer-like souls, who've gazed inspired on Truth's eternal
    forms,
That gleam unchanging, fair, divine, like stars above earth's
    storms ;
Who pant to lead mankind with you, Faith's Pisgah-steeps to
    climb,
Where man's great future dawns, unknown, far up Earth's
    coming time,
Take heart, fear not ; time's toil is long ; man's epochs, like the
    sphere's,
Swing slow through lab'ring centuries, or span a thousand
    years.
But Earth's old stratum-building powers are building strata
    still ;
And Truth, unspent in cycles past, still works God's mighty
    will.
Creation's archetypal thoughts, *life, righteousness,* and *love*
Work on through all the worlds below, and all the worlds
    above.

God's breath, that erst o'er chaos moved, when Nature's pulse
    grew warm,
Still breathes through every human age the life-gale of *reform.*
In every age God's spirit stirs, and wakens souls sublime,
Who light the beacon fires along the mountain-tops of time !
I see their flash, from peak to peak, along the ages hoary,
And catch the gathering thunder-swell of man's redemption-
    story !
From every opening sky of earth are heavenly voices crying,
And seer-like souls from clime to clime, in every tongue
    replying.
God's Spirit, breathed through all the world, reproves, awakes,
    enlightens,
Till Conscience dawns in savage breasts, as Revelation
    brightens ;
And he who worships God, and does the right, in every nation,
Accepted stands with heaven, and shares the Spirit's inspi-
    ration. [1]
From Enoch, Noah, Abraham, and Amram's mighty son,
The Tishbite grand, and he who stood on Mars' proud hill, and
    won ;
To him who smote the Scarlet Whore, and two, whose tongue
    and lyre,
Inspired by God, set England first, and then the world, on fire ;
Heroes by hosts, unnamed, unsung, with names the world
    shall cherish
When Fame's eternal brass is dust, and pyramids shall
    perish !

[1] Acts 10 : 35.

Through each, through all, one baptism flames, one impetus
    divine ;
Nor these alone, but souls who've groped, unlit by Salem's
    shrine ;
Cathay's great sage ; and India's seers, who sang in Vedic
    dawn ;
And Zendic Zerdusht, rapt to heaven from hoary, dim Irân ;
And he who kindled Asia's Light, renouncing crown and
    throne
To teach the world that he who serves is great, and he alone ;
The blind old bard whose matchless song from Greece o'er
    earth has rolled ;
The Hemlock's Martyr ; and thy name, Academy, untold !

II.

All heaven-born hero-souls are God's torch-bearers for
    mankind ;
But brightest they who most have caught his own all-kindling
    mind.
From Calvary's height Redemption's light shall shine o'er
    earth abroad,
But no true soul, from pole to pole, e'er cried in vain to God.
Truth, nature, mind, are steps to God ; he framed their
    radiant stair,
And he who climbs where God hath led shall find him every-
    where.
His wheels flash out on all earth's heights where souls in
    anguish call ;

Where'er faith dares the world for him, his fires responsive
    fall ;
New Baals vex each land and age, and new Ashérahs vile
Hunt Virtue's life with shameless strife, and many a secret
    wile ;
But God still sends his hero-souls to smite them with his rod,
For God's own Son man's victory won ; he reigns, the Hero-
    God !
He reigns ! And earth rolls nearer God, through long up-
    struggling ages,
With every hero sent by him, whose name illumes her pages ;
For *God in man brings man to God*, through faith, and love, and
    sorrow,
And toil and strife, that lift the world up toward a brighter
    morrow.
And souls that fight the fight for man, though shamed,
    defeated, broken,
Like weeping clouds are crowned at last with victory's rain-
    bow token.
Their names are set like steadfast stars in heaven's eternal
    arches,
To guide the pilgrimage of souls through all time's toiling
    marches.
And blest are they to whom the gift ineffable is given,
Through tears, through toils, through martyr fires, to light
    men on to heaven !

BROOKLYN, 1870—1885.   768 iambic septemeters.

THE CALLING OF MOSES.

[Book of Exodus, chapters 3, 4.]

I.

WHERE Midian's hoary mountains in rugged grandeur climb,
And rule her desert solitudes in majesty sublime,
Through lonely wilds and gorges, by springs among the rocks,
The exiled seer, a shepherd, led his roving, browsing flocks.

II.

At last on giant Horeb amid his charge he trod,
And roamed alone, with reverent feet, the awful Mount of
    God ;
Below lay green oases, above rose granite towers,
And all the soundless silence thrilled instinct with heavenly
    powers.

III.

Here, through long days of summer, among his lambs he
    strayed,
And pondered God's strange mysteries, wrestled and dreamed
    and prayed :
" Why all these years of exile, with Israel crushed the while ?
Why sleeps the wrath of Abraham's God above the trembling
    Nile ?

IV.

"If once God's spirit moved me in years so long ago
To save my downtrod race and strike the swift, delivering
    blow,
Why triumphs still the oppressor? Why yet doth Israel's cry
Rise, wild with anguish, yet bring down no voice from all the
    sky?"

V.

He ceased. A sudden wonder before his vision came!
Along the mountain thicket rose a strange and scathless flame!
Above the tangled hawthorn it leaped, as from a pyre,
And wrapped the unscorched copse, and towered a tent of
    lambent fire!

VI.

Then gazed the seer, astonished, to view the wondrous scene,
When lo! Jehovah's solemn voice, from out the blazing screen
Spake: "Moses! Moses!" Trembling he answered: "Here
    am I."
"Put off thy shoes, on holy ground, and hither draw not nigh!

VII.

"I am El-Shaddai,[1] mighty, the God of Abraham,
Of Isaac, Jacob, and thy sire, Jehovah, the I AM!
The cry of Israel's children has reached my throne on high;
I know their heavy sorrows, all, their woe and agony.

---

[1] Hebrew *El*, the Strong one, the common noun for God, and *Shaddai*,
Irresistible, translated "God Almighty," by *Murphy*, *Gen.* 17 : 1, the great
name by which God revealed himself to Abraham.

VIII.

" I am come down to save them from Egypt's bloody hand,
To smite the dire oppressor's power and scourge his guilty
     land ;
My arm, outstretched in wonders, shall make his realm a
     grave,
For earth and sea shall fight for me till I have freed the slave.

IX.

" I know thy own brave spirit, I love the heart that yearns
To rend the bondage of its kind, the fiery soul that burns
At others' wrong and outrage ; and, scorning power and
     pelf,
Dare rise for right 'gainst all earth's might, nor plan nor care
     for self.

X.

" But he who with Jehovah would fight the fight for man
Must wait till God reveal his rod and show the battle's plan ;
And forty years I've taught thee to meekly bide his time
Whose footsteps down earth's centuries beat one eternal rhyme.

XI.

" Rise, therefore, now, a hero in meekness as in might,
And I will send thee, thunder-clad, to shake the world for
     right.
But see thou aye remember the battle is not thine ;
Face thou the blame, the jeers, the shame, but count the
     victory mine.

XII.

"Lean on my arm, almighty, when sorrows bear thee down :
Fall back on me when flesh is weak and earth and demons
     frown.
God rules to-day, to-morrow ; God rules on earth, on high ;
And on his side all Heaven shall ride, all Hell before him fly !

XIII.

"Go now, meet haughty Egypt ; meet Pharaoh on his throne ;
Meet Israel's coward doubts and fears ; meet all, and shrink
     from none.
Take thou nor sword nor sceptre, thy might is all in me ;
Take only this, thy shepherd's staff, power in humility."

XIV.

Then rose the seer and hero, no more to fear or flee,
Instinct and conscious of his God, himself half deity !
Nations and Nature owned him and earth and time obey,
For he who does and dares in God, with God shall reign for aye.

XV.

For Right shall reign while kingdoms and empires are no
     more,
And civilizations ebb and flow like tides on ocean's shore ;
And he who'll lose the world for Right, with Right the world
     shall gain,
And linked with Truth and Right, in God, forever shine and
     reign.

THE DESTRUCTION OF EGYPT'S FIRST-BORN.

[Book of Exodus, chapter 12 : 29, 30.]

I.

WHAT wail was that which rose from Egypt's land,
  A wild and long and heart-appalling cry
  That smote the brazen arches of the sky
Upon that awful morning, when God's hand,
In vengeance terrible, had waved the brand,
  The viewless, soul-dissevering sword of wrath,
  O'er all her homes, and with its noiseless scath
Had touched and sundered every vital band
That bound her first-born life, unbound at his command !

II.

Egypt stood staggering in that shock of woe,
  Amazed, o'erwhelmed, till that wild wail went up,
  As to her quivering lips was pressed a cup
Whose withering agony can no man know
Who has not reeled in darkness while the throe
  Of that same great bereavement stabbed his soul
  With mortal anguish, which, o'er all control,
Burst in one black, bewildering, whelming flow,
That drove him drunk with grief, stunned, stifled by the blow.

III.

O Egypt ! Egypt ! such a woe was thine !
  And down the dim, long ages that have sped,
  I see thee stooping o'er thy prostrate dead,
In that dumb agony, while ominous shine
The clouds of morn, all blotched with bloody wine,
  As though the Hebrew rite were sprinkled there,
  As though o'er all the sky, and earth, and air,
In blood were written bold that awful sign
Of retribution dread, and mercy all divine !

IV.

In slavery's hut and haughty grandeur's hall,
  In regal dome, in stall, and open field,
  Alike did Death his iron sceptre wield,
And over all the land a fearful pall
Was spread, and spectral shadows, dark and tall,
  Moved up and down her palaces and streets,
  And goblin forms, in mouldy winding-sheets,
Unsummoned by the Magian's powerless call,
Sighed as they glided dim, by column, court, and wall.

V.

Manhood stood mute, in awe and terror dumb ;
  But woman's heart broke down beneath her love,
  In wild and passionate wailings, that might move
The hearts of marble sphinxes, cold and numb ;

And glorious, dark-eyed creatures, in the gloom
  Of Pharaoh's palace, on its floor of stone,
  Lay frantic flung, clasping with plaintive moan,
Their stiffening offspring, smitten by the doom
That made that gorgeous pile one vast and mournful tomb.

VI.

Thus Mizraim mourned : but all through Goshen's land,
  Where Israel's tribes beneath the blood-sign dwelt,
  No wailing rose. Awake and clad, they knelt,
Girded and shod, and ready, staff in hand,
For instant march, when came God's swift command.
  Their first-born, safe, with all their households spared,
  The paschal lamb with awe and wonder shared ;
While each glad father numbered all his band ;
And not a watch-dog howled, as though a ghost he scanned.

VII.

O Egypt ! Egypt ! say what was thy crime,
  That God should bruise thee in his anger so,
  And pour the baptism of such fearful woe
On thy proud head, and make thee, through all time,
A sad and awful monument sublime
  Of wrath and shame, of judgment and of fear,
  To all the ages, ever known and near,
Teaching a startling lore to every clime,
That thrills us like a knell with ever-echoing chime ?

VIII.

O Egypt ! Egypt ! let thy grandeur tell,
  Thy pyramids and sphinxes, for they can,
  How, age by age, they rose on bones of man !
And let the deep, dread echoes rise and swell
From labyrinth, and catacombs, where dwell
  Dead generations !   One eternal groan
  Comes up from every hewn and sculptured stone,
That answers too significantly well,
How Slavery's curse, through time, has made Nile's vale
      a hell !

IX.

O ye who rear on unrewarded toil
  The glory of a nation or an age,
  Know well a curse is writ on every page
Of every history of wrong and spoil !
It brands the brow, the soul, the very soil
  Of the oppressor with Jehovah's ban ;
  And all the luxury wrung from wrong to man,
And all the greatness reared on Freedom's foil,
Shall sink by slow decay, or sudden swift recoil !

THE PASSAGE OF THE RED SEA.

[Book of Exodus, chapters 14 and 15 ; Psalm 18 : 7-17.]

On land's remotest verge the bondmen stood,
And gazed, dismayed, upon the boundless flood.
Black, threatening mountains walled the arid shore,
The sea swept on, unbridged and waste before ;
And far and hoarse along the desert strand,
The long, loud billows beat the bending sand.

Now, mingling deep with ocean's ceaseless sound,
A muffled murmur steals along the ground,
Swelling like smothered thunder far behind,
Waxing and sinking with the western wind.
But anxious ears have caught the creeping jar
That loads the land-breeze with the tread of war,
And million hearts beat quick in deadly fear
As rolls the laboring discord yet more near.
In that dread hour a thousand memories roam
Back o'er the way that led them from their home—
That home of bondage, shame, oppression, pain,
Sorrow and sin—and quailing ones would fain
Fly from the present to the past again.
Was it that where we sorrow most, the heart

Makes e'en its tortures of its life a part?
Was it that age, and infancy, and love
Bring e'en to slavehood radiance from above?
Oh! ring not shrill along their ears the while,
The shrieks of infants from the waves of Nile?
Yet, O Death! Death! from thee, from *thee* we fly,
And oft we loathe to live, but dare not die!

But while such thoughts and darker throng their souls,
The far-off rumble near and nearer rolls,
Till, through the eddying dust-clouds, on their sight
Bursts a long line of plumes and helmets bright,
And sunset flames on banner, lance and spear,
Where Egypt's chariots flash in full career!

One wild, amazed and agonizing cry
Instant from Israel's armies smites the sky!
On God in terror million voices call,
On Moses million imprecations fall!
"Were there no graves in Egypt, that we flee
To perish in the wilderness with thee?
Did we not bid thee leave us there alone,
To serve th' Egyptians till our days were done?
Why hast thou thus our hearts and hopes beguiled,
And led us forth to slaughter in the wild!"
"Fear not," cried he, whose heaven-assisted hand
Had filled with woe and wonder Pharaoh's land;
"Stand still and see salvation from the Lord,
Revealed from heaven to prove his changeless word;

For these your foes, whom now your eyes deplore,
Henceforth shall vex your vision nevermore !"
  Still as they trembling gazed on foe and flood,
Fell from the skies the awful voice of God :
" Wherefore this cry of faithless fear to me !
Bid Israel forward ! Stretch above the sea
Thy hand, and lift thy rod to cleave its flow,
And lead my chosen through its depths below ;
And Egypt's king shall know that I am God,
What time I whelm him with the gulfing flood !"

  So spake Jehovah. Swift his Angel turns,
And o'er their rear the fiery pillar burns :
On Egypt frowning black with gloomiest night,
On Israel scattering soft serenest light.
Lo ! by its ray, at beck of Moses' rod,
The sea sinks down, as at the feet of God !
The east wind ploughs its billows like a share,
Furrowing the brine till ocean's bed is bare,
Flinging the foamy ridges long and high
On right and left, until they wash the sky ;
And emerald ranges, wreathed with rainbows, stand
Guarding a valley scooped by God's right hand !
  Down, down the gorge, far sloping from the shore,
The trembling millions now obedient pour,
Dry shod and safe along the yawning caves,
'Twixt mountain walls of piled and solid waves !
'Round the bared sand-spit stretched beyond their sight,

The chained abysses roar on left and right ;
And wave-worn rocks and coral groves they pass,
And strange sea-monsters glare through walls like glass.
The dreaded octopus waves all his arms,
And the coy mermaid shows her mingled charms ;
The great dugong goes plunging through the brine,
The dolphins gambol, and the sea-stars shine ;
And worm-gnawed ribs of foundered navies stand
Like giant bones half hid in ooze and sand !
Awed by such wonders Israel's myriads move
'Neath watery bastions looming dim above ;
While bright behind them—blackness to their foes—
The dread Shekinah like a meteor glows,
Cheers all the wasteful deep with dusky rays,
But lights their path with bright, benignant blaze.

But as they march adown the dread profound,
Their foiled pursuers catch the lessening sound,
And instant arm, with Heaven-sent fury blind,
And rush impetuous down the deep behind.

There is a point, a limit in all sins,
Where reason ends, and madness, stark, begins—
Where Heaven withdraws all judgment, shame or fear,
And retribution then is swift and near.
The impious wretch, to whom in vain are lent
All days of mercy, and all warnings sent
Whose soul, insensate, mocks where demons quail,
And scorns repentance till forbearance fail,
Sees, when too late, the bolt of vengeance gleam,
And drops, a blackened ruin, from his dream.

The nation that can crush a weaker race,
Or hunt the human kind like beasts of chase,
Be it by armies, hounds, or laws more fell,
Hangs toppling on the crumbling verge of hell !
And though she lift her haughty head alone,
Confronting Heaven with brow of slave-hewn stone,
Impatient thunders, big with fearful trust,
Tremble to leap and dash her into dust ;
And though Heaven's judgments linger and seem slow,
Not lighter falls the long-suspended blow
That hurls at last the blasted tyrant low !

O Egypt ! art thou not enough chastised ?
Is not thy pride by ten dire plagues advised ?
Rush not vague terrors on thy shrinking sight
From out the pall that doubles nature's night ?
Runs not along thy soul that wail untold
That rose, when morning found thy first-born cold ?
Seems not the burdened pressure of the air
To stir with whisperings bidding thee *forbear ?*
On, on they pour, by fiends exulting driven,
Smit with portentous hardihood from Heaven.
Throned in his burnished car the monarch rides,
Defiant gazing on the quivering tides,
That, with restraint impatient, creep, and move,
And curl, and hiss, and murmur far above.
On, on they pour, till now, in middle sea
The long black valley, open far and free,

Stretches before, behind, beyond their sight,
Where sky and ocean blend in circling night.

But as they rave along the hideous gloom,
Lo ! light appalling flashes on their doom !
Forth from the cloud in blinding blaze it streams,
Malignant influence rides on all its beams.
Perplexed, dismayed, all hearts with bodings quake ;
All arms relaxed in nerveless terror shake !
The steed, grown restive with brute instinct's dread,
Startles, and snorts, and flings his lofty head !
The trembling driver scarce his stand maintains,
Plies the vain thong, and grasps the useless reins !
While through the awestruck ranks that baleful glare
Shoots nameless horror, trembling, and despair !
But still the maniac king pursues his prey,
Scorns every token, mocks at all dismay,
Till hands unseen, innumerous, deftly steal
The pins that fasten many a rapid wheel ;
Erring, they roll, confused, at Heaven's command,
And many a laboring axle ploughs the sand ;
While swift avenging angels o'er them crowd,
And Israel's God looks lightnings from the cloud !
That look untold, that mortal never saw
And lived, whose glance fills holiest heav'n with awe,
There through that dread Shekinah's dazzling rays,
In form and face which lightning's self outblaze—
To which white noontide's beams are blackest night—

One instant burst o'erwhelming on their sight !
  With pale recoil, amazed, appalled, they cry
" From dreadful Israel let us turn and fly !
Jehovah fights for them 'gainst Mizraim's host !
Turn we, and fly ! Fly ! Fly ! or all is lost !"
They wheel ! They fly ! Then from the cloudy gloom
Breaks instant forth the fiery storm of doom !
The sultry air explodes with lurid flash !
The stifling murk is cleft with gleam and crash !
Dread thunders boom ! The bellowing heavens descend !
Lightning and rain in blinding wrath contend !
Blackness and whirlwind, sky and ocean blend !
And ebbing tides returning rise and sweep
And whirl and foam along the roaring deep !
  Ah ! vain repentance, or of man or state,
That never comes, until it comes too late !
E'en as they wheel, lo ! Israel's ransomed host,
With dawn safe climbing free Arabia's coast !
Too late, too late, through middle seas they fly,
The hour of vengeance flushes all the sky !

  O Maid of Egypt ! vainly dost thou wait
Thy hero-lover at thy palace gate !
Vainly, with love's fond studiousness prepare
To crown him victor, and to deck his car !
Vainly do waiting hearts of pride and love,
Through all the land at every footfall move !
Their last, their utterest desolation flies

Shadowy and swift, along the ominous skies ;
Omens in art, in man, and nature blend,
And Egypt, dead, shows living Egypt's end !
The voiceless catacombs hear rumblings dread,
Where mummied kings and gods forsake their bed !
Colossal Memnon's tuneful statues groan,
And dateless sphinxes sweat through veins of stone !
The glyptic obelisks with terror nod,
And shuddering pyramids own Israel's God !
Ten direful plagues throughout the world proclaim
Jehovah's wrath at Slavery's wrong and shame :
One final stroke, stupendous and sublime,
Shall peal the Re-enslaver's doom through time !
For when God's right hand rends the bondman's chain,
Woe ! woe to him who'd weld the links again—
Who'd rashly brave th' Omnipotent's decree !
He wars with God, who wars with Liberty !

Once more wide sounds the awful voice of God ;
Once more wide waves the sea-compelling rod,
And, at its beck, the pent, impatient tide
In deluge-mountains bursts on either side !
Vainly in frantic terror from its flow,
Shoreward they rage, tumultuous, far below !
Before, behind, with instantaneous pour,
The ocean plunges and the surges roar !
Vainly at once to thousand gods they cry,
To prop the seas, that stooping, hide the sky !

Osiris, Isis, Apis, Mnevis, Rha,
Anubis, Ammon, Horus, Thoth, and Phtha,
The gods of Heaven and earth, of sea and sky,
Sun, moon, bull, ram, dog, crocodile, and fly,
Mind's loftiest visions, base and bestial forms,
Dreams of Eternity, cats, frogs, and worms—
What are they all, when dread Jehovah rolls
A wrathful ocean on their shuddering souls,
And Memphian chivalry, and Theban pride,
Kings, priests, and gods are whelmed beneath the tide !

With shock tremendous yields each quivering wall,
Immense and swift the sea-green arches fall,
And ruin runs with level lapse o'er all !
One moment, struggling in the surge for life,
See some strong swimmer stem the seething strife !
One moment Pharaoh's golden armor shines
'Mid cataracts booming like exploding mines !
One moment madly plunging in their toils,
His war-steeds flounder where the tumult boils ;
And one long, mingled, stifled, strangled scream
Comes like the gasp-shriek of a nightmare dream ;
And Pharaoh, deified, and prince, and slave,
Together sink beneath th' all-whelming wave ;
And meeting billows skip and clap their hands,
And laugh wild requiem o'er proud Egypt's bands,
That slumber low along the weltering sands ;
Egypt with all her power to ruin hurled !

A doom whose dread, whose fame, shall fill the world !
Far as Earth's shores extend, her oceans roll,
Through tropic climes or 'round each icy pole,
All tribes shall learn Jehovah's name t' adore,
The God whose love uplifts the humblest poor,
The awful God of Right forevermore !

THE SMITING OF THE ROCK IN KADESH

[Book of Numbers, chapter 20 : 1–13.]

I.

WATER ! no water ! rock and sand—
A weary, parched, and burning land ;
The springs all sunk—the torrents dry—
The clouds all perished from the sky !

II.

Zin seemed on fire, and Kadesh lay
Blasted beneath the torrid ray ;
No shadowy palms, nor herb, nor grass—
Earth, glowing iron—sky, blazing brass !

III.

The goat-skins, all their moisture spent,
Hung shrunk and crackling in each tent ;

And ghastly bands of frantic men
Searched vainly every grot and glen.

IV.

Then hoarse and deep along the plain
Gathered a sound of wrath and pain,
And loud the angry murmur burst
From millions mad with torturing thirst.

V.

" Is this the land our seers foretold,
Whose streams in milk and honey rolled ?
Whose woods and groves drip balm and oil ?
Whose harvests load the heaven-drenched soil ?

VI.

" Why have ye here God's people brought,
Us and our herds to slay for naught ;
Where never fruits nor vines were found,
And fountless deserts blaze around !

VII.

" Would God that when his instant ire
Wrapped Korah's host in sheeted fire,
We, too, had shared that pangless doom,
Or filled with them the earthquake tomb !"

VIII.

So raved the ingrates God had fed
With one long miracle of bread !

In prostrate agony of woe
God's seer held back Heaven's righteous blow.

IX.

Then flashed God's glory, pealed his word,
While awestruck thousands trembling heard
Jehovah's mandate, echoing wide,
Till listening caves and crags replied :

X.

" Take thou the rod ! the nation call !
Command yon cliff before them all !
And springs shall rise and streams shall burst,
Till man and nature slake their thirst."

XI.

Now, forth before th' expectant throng,
Erring, yet in God's mercy strong,
Lifting toward heaven the mystic rod,
Stands he who erst dread Sinai trod.

XII.

He smites.   The stern dark rock rebounds
The blow, and all the vale resounds ;
But all its secret springs unknown
Leap, startled, in their veins of stone !

XIII.

Again the prophet's arm descends ;
The conscious granite groans and rends,

And lo ! a fountain, silver fair,
Mounts flashing through the burning air !

XIV.

Wide through the camp glad voices cry,
And "Water !" "Water !" fills the sky ;
While rapturous thousands mingling rush
Where glittering rivulets foam and gush.

XV.

With brazen helm the warrior dips
The spouting nectar to his lips ;
The old man, trembling, bowed with years,
Thanks God, and drinks with reverent tears.

XVI.

The youth, half eager, half afraid,
Hands his full pitcher to the maid ;
The mother, in her thirst half wild,
First satisfies her youngest child.

XVII.

The bullock snuffs the freshening gale,
Bellows, and bounds along the vale ;
And cow and goat, and lamb and hound,
Quaff the cool rills that gurgle 'round.

XVIII.

The war-steed neighs, and champs his chain,
Then charges thundering down the plain ;

The patient camel breaks his fast,
And drinks, the longest, and the last.

XIX.

O Thou, the Rock of truth and Grace,
Once cleft to save a dying race,
Thy streams of mercy, full and free,
Still flow for all mankind and me.

XX.

O may we, like thy flock of old,
Drink deep from all thy springs untold ;
Nor e'er, like Israel, doubt the plan
Of God's unfailing love for man.

XXI.

Nor e'er, like him, God honored most,
Forget in whom is all our boast ;
And, once impatient, rash, and vain,
Lose Canaan here—and heaven scarce gain.

THE PASSAGE OF JORDAN.

[Book of Joshua, chapters 3, 4.]

I.

From Egypt's bloody bondage the ransomed seed had passed,
By flaming mounts and sundered seas, to Canaan's bounds, at
    last.
The land, from snow-crowned Hermon to Arnon's rushing
    wave,
Was won by him whom God's own hand had laid in glory's
    grave.

II.

And now Jehovah summoned to cross old Jordan's flood,
To Canaan, claimed four hundred years by deed from Abra-
    ham's God ;
A deed renewed to Isaac, to Jacob, Joseph too,
The land surveyed from Pisgah's top in Moses' glorious view.

III.

Ho ! God's great day is dawning ! Hark how the trumpets
    sound !
Till Moab's hills and echoing crags the stirring peals rebound !
The ordered tribes in beauty around their banners form,
And o'er God's tent the fiery cloud glows like a rainbowed
    storm !

IV.

Then first 'came princely Judah,[1] whose towering standard
  burned ;
And with him patient Issachar, and Zebulun the learned ;
And next marched first-born Reuben, with Simeon's fiery band,
And Gad's strong troop of mountaineers from Gilead's fra-
  grant land.

V.

And then came mighty Ephraim, Manasseh's double host,
And fierce left-handed Benjamin, who made the sling his boast ;
And last moved lion-hearted Dan, with Asher's wealthy horde,
And Naphtali, the fleet of foot and eloquent in word.

VI.

Before the host went Levi, to bear his sacred charge,
Jehovah's tabernacle dread, and stood by Jordan's marge ;
Before them rolled a raging tide from far-off Hermon's snows ;
For Jordan's flood, at harvest heat, his triple banks o'erflows.

VII.

On swept the swelling freshet, and high and higher clomb
The whirling, maddening chaos of fury and of foam ;
The majesty of Nature in her unbridled hour,
That mocks the insect might of man, and scorns his pigmy
  power.

---

[1] For the order of encampment and marching, in four grand divisions of
three tribes each, see Num. 2 ; and for the characteristics of the tribes, see
Jacob's blessing, Gen. 49 : 1–27, and Moses' blessing, Deut. 33 : 6–25 ; with
other passages.

VIII.

What!   Tempt that sea of surges ?—that turbid,wild abyss ?—
Dost hear the roar like thunder ?—the dash, and boil, and
   hiss ?
Go face the Red Sea's rolling !   Go brave the dread simoom !
But dare not swelling Jordan when all his torrents boom !

IX.

Then came Jehovah's answer : " This day will I begin
To magnify my captain, and bring my people in.
This day will I do wonders.   This day your fear and dread,
Through Canaan's trembling nations, in terror shall be
   spread."

X.

Then Joshua's trumpet sounded : " Take up Jehovah's
   shrine !
The Lord of all the earth goes forth to lead His covenant
   line !
March onward into Jordan !   Obey the living God !
Ye pass to-day an unknown way, by mortals never trod !"

XI.

The mighty column marches, the ark of God before ;
They wind down Moab's headlands, and stand by Jordan's
   roar ;
Jehovah's cloudy curtains float above the deluge, dim,
The sacred feet of white-haired priests are dipped in Jordan's
   brim.

XII.

Lo ! at that touch divided, as by an unseen sword,
From shore to shore the surges cleave a path for Nature's
     Lord !
Above, the headlong waters in heaps and mountains pile !
Below, the ebbing channel runs dry for many a mile ![1]

XIII.

Far up the rock-walled valley a refluent lake expands
Ten leagues, to Adam's city, that hard by Zarthan stands ;
While cliffs of quivering crystal, and foam like Alpine snow,
O'erhang, in awful cataracts, the yawning gulf below.

XIV.

But there Jehovah's altar and ark of mystic power,
Upborne on mortal shoulders, stand firm for many an hour ;
While swiftly marching myriads, a mighty bannered host,
Sweep on from Moab's border, and cross to Canaan's coast.

XV.

O thrilling scene, stupendous !   Far as the eye can gaze,
I hear the tramp of millions, and see their standards' blaze !
I hear the pealing trumpets, the clarions' glad reply !
The shouts of joy and wonder that shake the arching sky !

---

[1] The channel below the miraculous dam would rapidly run dry, leaving
room for the column to cross with a front several miles wide, which would
be necessary, in order that nearly three millions of people, with their cattle
and property, should cross in one day.

XVI.

I see Jehovah's promise to Abraham, his "friend,"
Through four dark centuries of strife remembered to the end ;
And these are Abraham's children ! To-day their millions
    come,
With matchless might and miracle, to claim their long-sought
    home !

XVII.

The wondrous march is over—still Judah in the van ;
While, proud to guard the dangerous rear, comes firm and
    valiant Dan ;
And now on Canaan's headlands and beetling bluffs they form,
To view God's work accomplished, where man is but a worm.

XVIII.

Lo, now, twelve giant warriors, from every standard one,
Stand there in Jordan's deepest bed, and heave each man a
    stone,
A massive, wave-worn boulder, on every shoulder strong,
They bear, to tell this glorious day through unborn ages long.

XIX.

And where God's priests stood steadfast beneath the dreadful
    height
Of live waves curling far o'erhead, and quivering in their
    sight,
There twelve huge, ponderous masses in ordered pile they lay,
God's rock-built trophy in the deep, his witness to this day.

XX.

And now the wonder-working Ark the white-haired pontiffs
      guide ;
They climb the slippery steep, and touch dry land, on Ca-
      naan's side ;
The bridled floods have waited the end of God's command,
And instant leap, unfettered, from his relaxing hand.

XXI.

With towering curve, majestic, the watery mountains bend !
The liquid precipice o'erhangs, one arch, from end to end !
Then boom ten thousand thunders !   Ten thousand cataracts
      roar !
And tumbling, seething chaos foams and bounds from shore
      to shore !

XXII.

Down the long gorge vast rollers in white-maned squadrons
      sweep,
Like Ukraine's wild battalions,[1] or like the billowy deep,
The glad, the fierce, the glorious, the thund'rous war of
      waves,
When all the rout of storms is out, and all the tempest raves !

XXIII.

The long lake bursts in grandeur along its craggy way,
It shoots and leaps and dashes, and flies in glittering spray ;

---

[1] Ukraine's wild battalions, the famous herds of wild horses of the Ukraine,
or Cossack Russia.
  " A tartar of the Ukraine breed."   Byron's " Mazeppa."

For Jordan the Descender, with tumult loud and hoarse,
In all his rage goes plunging adown his ancient course.

XXIV.

Each summer through the ages, o'er all his banks once more,
Rolls Jordan's freshet-fury, resistless as of yore,
But ever, while earth's rivers pour their endless hymn to God,
Shall this be told, how Israel crossed old Jordan's flood, dry-
shod.

XXV.

So ever, when God's chosen march on in dauntless faith,
And trust his might, and do and dare with Him, in life or
death,
Shall rock still gush with fountains, and seas and rivers fly,
Till man and nature join the soul inspired for victory.

XXVI.

And ever when the Canaanite is mighty to oppose,
Jehovah's deathless victories shall awe his quaking foes,
And tower as blazing beacons his conquering hosts to fire,
Whose march sublime, through earth and time, still seeks a
kingdom higher.

XXVII.

March on, my soul, undaunted, where duty shines before,
Though deserts blaze around thee, and Jordans surge and
roar.
The land on this side Jordan is not thy birthright blest,
March on and find thy Canaan, and enter into rest.

THE OVERTHROW OF JERICHO.

[Book of Joshua, chapters 5 and 6.]

I.

HARK !—that shock ! that crash ! whose thunder
   Rolls from Jordan's vale profound !—
Fills the echoing hills with wonder !—
   Awes the Amorite regions 'round !—
Rolls through far-off lands and nations !—
   Swells through listening earth and time !—
Told through endless generations !—
   Sung in many a song sublime !—

II.

When o'er Jordan's flood, affrighted,
   Israel's host had crossed dry-shod ;
And the soil to Abraham plighted
   Abraham's ransomed children trod ;—
There, athwart their march, defiant,
   Ruling far the plain below,
On her rock-walled strength reliant,
   Frowned the far-famed JERICHO.

III.

'Round those ramparts, gray and hoary,
   Hosts have raged in many a fight,

Bards have sung her power and glory ;
  Kings have owned her conquering might.
Wealth of realms and lore of ages
  In her storied halls are found ;
Priests and pontiffs, seers and sages,
  Temples, altars, shrines, abound.

IV.

O'er her tower her guardian mountains ;
  Round her wave her groves of palm ;
At her foot her murmuring fountains
  Lave the balsam, spice, and balm.
On through fields and groves they wander,
  Where her tropic breezes [1] blow,
Fringed with cane and oleander ;—
  Lovely, fragrant Jericho ! [2]

V.

But o'er all her power and splendor
  Hangs a chill and palsying gloom ;
Gates and towers in vain defend her ;
  Dawns, foretold, her hour of doom !
Dark idolatries, unuttered,
  Blast her strength like scorching flame ;
All her prayers to fiends are muttered,
  All her shrines are marts of shame !

---

[1] On account of the great depth of the Jordan Valley below the level of the Mediterranean Sea, its climate is tropical.

[2] Jericho means place of fragrance, from its productions.

VI.

Baal, Lord of lust unbridled ;
  Foul Ashtoreth ; Moloch dire,
Hymned with shrieks of infants cradled
  In his brazen arms of fire !
Chemosh, served by base-born Ammon ;
. Midian's Peor, most obscene ;
Gods of blood and strife and mammon,
  Reign beneath her bowers of green.

VII.

Woe the day when soul or nation
  Sets corruption's throne on high !
Deifies abomination !
  Flaunts damnation to the sky !—
As the whirlwind's shade of terror
  Flies along the frightened world,
So th' avenging doom of error
  Hails Jehovah's sign unfurled !

VIII.

Lo, where Israel's warrior legions,
  Sore from circumcision's vow,
Helpless 'mid the foe's wide regions,
  Purged, before Jehovah bow !—   .
Abraham's sign on Abraham's nation ;
  Abraham's cov'nant all restored ;
Life-long excommunication
  Ended at Jehovah's word !

IX.

Lo, the Paschal lamb now bleeding,
  And the Paschal supper spread !
Memory back to Egypt speeding,
  And that night of woe and dread !
He who then spared Israel's dwellings,—
  He who smote the mightier foe,—
He who curbed old Jordan's swellings,—
  He shall smite proud Jericho !

X.

Israel, purged, in full communion
  Stands, a sacramental host ;
Both her sacraments in union,
  Speak Jehovah all her boast.
Where her ordered tribes are blending
  All is peace and pure accord ;
'Round their standards all attending
  Wait the mandate of the Lord.

XI.

Now, where Jericho stands warder
  O'er wide Jordan's plain below,
Buckler of the Amorite border,
  Joshua walks with studious brow ;—
Views those battlements amazing,
  Peers o'er fortress, moat and plain,
Marking, measuring, questioning, gazing,
  Pondering deep the great campaign.

XII.

Lo ! before his sight advancing
  See a mighty warrior stand !
See the sword, in sunbeams glancing,
  Brandished in his strong right hand !
All unarmed, in dress a yeoman,
  Bold the dauntless chief spake out,
"Art thou friend or art thou foeman ?
  Stand, and answer Israel's scout !"

XIII.

"Not at mortal challenge spoken,
  Here I stand !"—A light divine
O'er that visage flashed its token—
  Heaven's imperial countersign !—
"But as Captain here, revealing
  Dread Jehovah's battle plan,
Here I stand, my name concealing,
  Stand to guide my war for man !

XIV.

"Ask no more my name or nature !
  Loose thy shoe, on holy ground !"
Glory flashed from form and feature !—
  Prone, in prostrate awe profound,
Down the mortal fell, adoring !—
  "Lo, I wait, with Israel's band,
Heaven's all-conquering aid imploring !
  Let Jehovah give command !"

XV.

Then Jehovah, undissembling :—
   "Jericho e'en now is thine !
Earth shall hear her tale with trembling,
   Hear, and own the deed divine !
Doom to blanch the world with pallor
   Swift my fated hour shall bring !
Thine her mightiest men of valor,
   Thine her pontiffs, princes, king !'

XVI.

"Thine ;—but not by mortal daring,
   Not by mortal might o'erthrown ;
Mine the stroke, no mortal sharing,—
   Mine the fame, the spoil, alone.
Mine,—but far as spreads the story
   While the wondering world grows old,—
Long as lives Jehovah's glory,
   Shall your conquering faith be told.

XVII.

"Sound the stirring proclamation !
   Blow the trumpets, full and far !
Silver trumpets of salvation,
   Not the brazen clang of war !
Let the priests take up my coffer,
   Let the vanguard march before ;
Fear no sortie, heed no scoffer,
   Show your faith,—I ask no more !"

XVIII.

Lo, at morn the mighty column
  Moves from Gilgal, grand and slow !—
Mark the silence, stern and solemn !
  Hear the sacred clarions blow !
See the tribes from far o'er Jordan,
  Reuben, Gad, Manasseh strong,
Proud to share war's toil and guerdon,
  Armed and harnessed pour along !

XIX.

Next God's awful ark advances,
  Where the sevenfold trumpets peal ;—
Then the gathering host, where glances
  Sunrise o'er a sea of steel !
Tribes on tribes, no war-cry raising,
  Eye their standards from afar ;—
Each on high, resplendent blazing,
  Guides its myriads like a star !

XX.

On, and on, with tramp unbroken,
  Still the mustering myriads go !
On, with ne'er a whisper spoken,
  Moves their march 'round Jericho !
All her gates with rust corroding !—
  All her walls with gazers throng !—
Some with speechless, dire foreboding,
  Some with ribald jeer and song !

XXI.

Day by day that march stupendous
  'Round those silent gates has passed !—
Dawns the seventh, the day tremendous !—
  Dawns the day of doom at last !—
Lo, ere pales the star of morning,
  Gilgal's stirring cornets sound !—
Hosts on hosts, at that glad warning,
  Armed and shod, from bivouac bound !

XXII.

Hosts on hosts, well fed and furnished,
  Strong to dare the arduous day !
Hosts on hosts, in armor burnished ;
  War's magnificent array !
On, still on, the trumpets sounding,
  Lead the concourse 'round and 'round !
On, still on, their tramp resounding,
  Shakes with fear the solid ground !

XXIII.

Seven the priests, and seven the cornets ;
  Seven the days, the seventh day seven !—
Lamps and pitchers !—oxgoads !—hornets !—
  Such the weapons chosen by heaven !—
Sacred signs and mystic wonders
  Speak Jehovah's war begun ;
Seven apocalyptic thunders
  Hail at last the victory won !

XXIV.

Lo, the last day's sunlight lingers,
  Journeying down the western sky ;—
All its beams, like Fate's broad fingers,
  Point the awful instant nigh !
Still, as adamant unshaken,
  Stand those century-hardened walls !
Not a stone,—its bed forsaken,—
  Not a flake of mortar, falls !

XXV.

See, the last long round is ended ;
  See the marshalled legions stand,
In one mighty circle blended,
  Ranks on ranks, now sword in hand !
They who fed on heavenly manna,—
  They who humbled Jordan trod,—
Wait to thunder dread Hosannah,
  At the mandate of their God !

XXVI.

Hark ! God's solemn proclamation
  Claims the treasures he shall win ;
Claims the first-fruits of the nation,
  Ere his onset shall begin !
" Woe to him who robs his Maker !
  Him shall earth and Heaven confound !
Blest is he, with God partaker !—
  Let the sevenfold trumpets sound !"

XXVII.

Hark ! That sevenfold peal, resounding !
  Long and loud its echoes fly !—
Hark ! that myriad shout, rebounding,
  Rolls along the vaulted sky !
Rolls in more than mortal volume !
  Booms like ocean's bursting swell !
Rolls o'er wall, and arch, and column !
  Shakes yon inmost citadel !

XXVIII.

Sight amazing !—shock astounding !—
  See those granite ramparts rise !
Heaved and tossed like waves, confounding
  Towers and bulwarks in the skies !
Walls and warriors mingled falling !
  Strong defenders, and their trust !
All, with yell and roar appalling,
  Crashing, thundering to the dust !

XXIX.

Not like floods o'er lowlands streaming,—
  Not like whirlwind's whelming rush,—
Not the lightning's red bolt gleaming,—
  Not the earthquake's roll and crush,—
Here Jehovah sent no servant !
  Here he bared his own right hand !
Answering faith so pure and fervent
  With one touch that shook the land.

XXX.

Lo ! where, o'er the chaos 'round it,
    Still one splintered turret towers !
Lo ! the nest-like house that crowned it,
    Safe as rocked in summer bowers !
From its window, bright unfolding,
    Flutters Rahab's scarlet cord !
God's right hand, that spire upholding,
    Owns and keeps his covenant word !

XXXI.

Ho ! the lofty ladders, bending,
    Rise amid the murky air !
Ho ! with thankful haste ascending,
    Mount the spies erst sheltered there !
Rahab, saved, with father, mother,
    Downward tremble, round by round,
All her kindred, every brother,
    Stand, at last, on solid ground !

XXXII.

Saved !—One shout of generous gladness
    Thrills that war-worn veteran host !
Lightening o'er war's wreck and madness
    Beams, the brighter for their cost !—
Ho ! once more the clarions pealing !
    Ho ! the clash of sword and targe !
Ho ! where glittering cohorts, wheeling,
    Shout Jehovah's final charge !

XXXIII.

Inward draws the awful cordon !
  Onward sweeps th' embattled line !
Serried files resistless poured on,
  In an avalanche divine !
On o'er prostrate walls and arches,
  Towers and temples heaped and hurled,
On, each conquering column marches,
  On, as o'er a ruined world !

XXXIV.

Sword and spear and lance and arrow
  Sweep in steely tempest 'round !
Narrower still, and yet more narrow,
  Shrinks that deadly circle's bound !
Vain the foeman's charge and sally !
  Vain the Amorite gods implored !
Vain proud Jericho's last rally,
  'Gainst the charge of Israel's Lord !

XXXV.

Hark, where Israel's proud Hosannas
  Loud and long in triumph ring !
Down go squadrons ! Down go banners !
  Down go pontiffs, princes, king !—
Victory ! Victory for Jehovah !
  Canaan's bestial gods o'erthrown
Point the day when all earth over
  Christ shall reign, and Christ alone !

XXXVI.

Lo, what piles of spoil and treasure,
    Gleaned from subject lands and towns !—
Silver heaped like corn, by measure !
    Gold and jewels, gems and crowns !
Altar, temple, shrine and palace
    Yield up many a sumless hoard ;
Many a glittering robe, and chalice,
    Swell the store for Israel's Lord.

XXXVII.

Lo ! where funeral torches, flaring,
    Light a city's blood-red pyre !—
'Mid the dusk of evening glaring,
    Onward rolls the storm of fire !
More and more the vast cremation
    Surging, roaring, mounts on high !—
Earth a sea of conflagration !—
    Surf of flame that sweeps the sky !

XXXVIII.

All is o'er !—Yon dying embers,
    Reddening all the midnight dome,
Write a tale that earth remembers
    Through millenniums to come !
Write Jehovah's retribution,
    Emblem of eternal wrath !—
Write one sinner's absolution,—
    Saved by faith from sin and death !

XXXIX.

Aye, they write how God's campaigning
  High o'er mortal wisdom shines ;—
Earthly arms and arts disdaining ;—
  Conquering on celestial lines !
When the soul, the church, the nation,
  Dares to trust him, and obey,
Fools may scoff, but God's salvation
  Waits along th' appointed way.

XL.

When, in heartfelt consecration,
  Searching all the soul within,
Faith, through one great expiation,
  Claims the death of inbred sin,—
Then that miracle supernal,
  Life divine through Christ, is given,
Life in God, complete, eternal ;
  Canaan here,—the dawn of heaven.

XLI.

Thus when Israel, purged and kneeling,
  Waits the Captain of God's host,—
Waits in faith the all-revealing,   `
  All-anointing Holy Ghost,—
Then shall flash the fiery token !
  Then shall gleam the Spirit's sword !
Then from mortal lips be spoken,
  Clothed with might, the Living Word !

XLII.

Then the church shall know her orders,
    By her Great Commander given ;
Bold shall claim the earth's wide borders,
    Every foe before her driven ;—
'Round the world her trumpets sounded,—
    Every Jericho o'erthrown,—
Every hostile power confounded,—
    Christ shall reign from zone to zone !

XLIII.

Know, O Church, thy circumcision,
    Though earth's dearest pleasures pall !
Then march on, 'mid earth's derision,
    Wheresoe'er God's trump shall call.
Haste, O Christ, that crash of thunder
    When earth's hoary errors fall !
When all realms yon blue heaven under,
    Own Jehovah Lord of all.

XLIV.

"Haste, O Christ !"   Thy saints are crying,
    "Haste and lead thy chosen on !"
Hark ! a heavenly voice replying—
    "Fall'n is mighty Babylon !"
Jericho's campaign is ended !
    Antichrist's dominion past !
Heathen powers, that long contended,
    Ope their gates to Christ at last.

XLV.

India's hoary systems totter !
China's walls no more oppose !
Bright Japan, Old Ocean's daughter,
  Hails her teachers, erst her foes !
Afric, from her darkest center
  Spreads her arms like Congo's flood,—
Bids her " Pauline Bishop" [1] enter,—
Welcomes hosts that work for God !

XLVI.

Earth, explored, espied like Canaan,
  Soon, like Canaan shall be won ;
Moslem, Brahmin, Boodhist, Pagan,
  All shall bow, and kiss God's son.
JOSHUA, JESUS, goes before us,
  Where yon blood-stained banner flies !
Canaan 'round, within, and o'er us ;—
  Endless Canaan in the skies !

---

[1] Bishop William Taylor, of the Methodist Episcopal Church, Missionary Bishop for Africa, and the greatest mission-founder of this generation, who is at this moment (May 1885) entering Africa from both shores with about forty missionaries, to draw a cordon of missionary posts across the continent, along the southern watershed of the recently explored Congo.

GIDEON'S CAMPAIGN.

Part I. The Sword of the Lord and of Gideon.

[Book of Judges, chapters 6, 7.]

I.

" The sword of the Lord and of Gideon !" rose
The watch-cry at midnight o'er Israel's foes—
A cry that has rung since the night of its birth,
Through the nations of men and the ages of earth.

II.

Ah, sad was the thraldom of Israel's race,
Invaded and plundered, in woe and disgrace !
The land was in mourning, the cities in dread,
And village and hamlet despair overspread.

III.

For Israel's seed had forgotten the Lord,
And bowed to vain idols and Baals abhorred,
And the wrath of Jehovah has hissed for the foe,
And bade the destroyer the land overflow.

IV.

And Midian is there with his camels untold,
And Amalek, fierce in his onset of old,
With the sons of the desert, and tribes of the East,
On Israel's fatness like locusts to feast.

V.

Like waves the wild raiders in fury have pressed
From the hills of the East to the plains of the West,
From Gilead to Gaza Arabia's horde
Has ravaged and wasted the land of the Lord.

VI.

The ruthless marauder still riots and raves,
And Israel crouches in dens and in caves ;
No arm to deliver, no leader, no rest,
Robbed, ravished, and hunted, harassed and distressed.

VII.

Then Israel cried in her anguish to God,
Bewailing her sins, and confessing his rod ;
And God sent his prophet his people to chide
For their Amorite gods, their rebellion, and pride.

VIII.

And then came God's angel, and sat 'neath the oak
Of Joash, in Ophrah, that grew by the rock,
In the vale, by the winepress, where, hid from the foe,
The wheat sheaves rebounded the thresher's strong blow.

IX.

Then clear, o'er the thunder of flail after flail,
The voice of the angel swelled out on the gale,
And bade valiant Gideon rise in his might,
And lead forth God's armies to battle for right.

X.

" Jehovah is with thee, thou hero !" he cried.
" Ah, Lord, who am I," the meek farmer replied ;
" In lowly Manasseh my father is poor,
And I am the least of his household obscure !"

XI.

" Nay, rise in this might of thy meekness, and go,
And myriads shall fall as one man at thy blow !
Jehovah hath sent thee, his word cannot fail,
And Midian shall fly as the chaff from thy flail !"

XII.

Then sacrifice smoked at the angel's consent,
Flame leaped from the rock at his touch as he went,
Ascending he vanished ; God's servant, new-fired
For duty and freedom, rose rapt and inspired.

XIII.

Then fell Baal's altar and image by night !
Then Joash, converted, grows bold for the right,
Defies the wild mob, and defends his brave son !
Abi-ezer is purged, and God's triumph begun.

XIV.

Then echoes God's trump through the tribes of the North,
And Zebulon, roused at the summons, springs forth,
And Asher and Naphtali, fired at the word,
Are joined with Manasseh to war for the Lord.

XV.

Then back to Jehovah flies Gideon again,
For signs and for strength in the doubtful campaign ;
And the fleece in the floor, wet or dry, as he prays,
Proclaims triumph waiting, and chides his delays.

XVI.

Then came God's strange mandate to winnow the host—
Already too few—lest vain Israel boast
" My arm won the fight !" and the cravens at heart,
The base, the exempts, twenty thousand, depart !

XVII.

Then He who reads hearts, and hides glory from men,
Said, " Yet they're too many, sift Israel again !
Sound the charge !" And nine thousand seven hundred bow
    low,
And drink long, at the brook, for they quail at the foe !

XVIII.

But three hundred heroes, with spirits aflame
For the glory of God, and at Israel's shame,
Scarce lap from their hands, as they bound o'er the ford,
And charge on the foe, in the wrath of the Lord.

XIX.

" Take those," said Jehovah ; " the rest to their tents !
Give me men of fire, who are done with laments,
Whose souls leap for action, with ardor aglow,
Like the spark from the steel, or the shaft from the bow !

XX.

" By those will I save you ; in them is the stuff
God's heroes are made of ; with God they're enough
To scatter proud Midian like leaves in the gale :
But now, in such strain, if thy courage should fail,

XXI.

Take Purah, thy servant, go down to the host,
And learn from themselves that already they're lost,
'Ere a sword has been drawn !"   Trembling Gideon obeys,
And the dreams they are telling the listeners amaze.

XXII.

" A barley loaf tumbled among us this night,
And smote a huge tent, and o'erturned it outright,"
Said one ; said another, " This loaf is the son
Of Joash the farmer, and Midian's undone !"

XXIII.

O'erawed at God's token, the hero returns ,
Strange ardor within him like prophecy burns :
" Arise ! for Jehovah hath given the sign,
And Midian is doomed by an omen Divine !"

XXIV.

The torches in pitchers are lighted in haste,
The trumpets are grasped, and the brave bands are placed ;
Around each vast camp, one weak hundred, they stand,
But heaven's bright seraphim wait the command.

XXV.

Then broke on the midnight the sudden loud crash !
Then blazed through the midnight the lightning-like-flash !
Then pealed through the midnight the trumpets' fierce clang,
Till rocks, hills, and caverns re-echoing rang !

XXVI.

Then " *The Sword of the Lord and of Gideon !*" rose
The watch-cry of terror o'er Israel's foes ;
From hundred to hundred thrills onward the cry,
From mountain to mountain the echoes reply !

XXVII.

Gilboa's rough crags to the clangor resound !
From wild little Hermon the trumpets rebound !
Till " *The Sword of Jehovah and Gideon !*" rolls
Like thunders of doom from the sky to the poles !

XXVIII.

But hark ! what wild clamor now swells from the vale !
Rage, terror, and agony ! Anger and wail !
And outcry, and clashing, and trampling, and roar,
Like torrents, or waves on the storm-beaten shore !

XXIX.

Yells ! shouts of command ! shrieks of frenzy and fear !
Rise dire o'er the clatter of armor and spear,
And wild squadrons rush without order or form,
Like clouds in the whirlwind, or ships in the storm !

XXX.

'Tis the arm of Jehovah made bare in his wrath !
'Tis the glare of his lightning, the gleam of its scath !
For the " *Sword of the Lord* " from its scabbard has leapt,
And armies like corn in its compass are reapt !

XXXI.

And Midian and Amalek, partners in spite,
Like stubble are swept by his besom of might,
And the sword of Manasseh, and Gideon's shout,
Still rage on their rear through the night of the rout !

XXXII.

Down Jezreel's dark valley the doom-maddened host
Like foam, on red billows of carnage, is tost,
Till Ephraim springs, like a lion in power,
To the fords of the Jordan, to rend and devour !

XXXIII.

There the steeds of the desert, the camel's tall pride,
And their riders, are swept on the gore-purpled tide,
And Oreb and Zeeb, with their princes, go down,
At the rock and the winepress to ghastly renown.

XXXIV.

O Sword of the Lord and of Gideon ! what light,
What glory unfading, has streamed from that night,
When three hundred heroes, with this for their cry,
Stood up for Jehovah, to conquer or die !

XXXV.

The three hundred Spartans,[1] who guarded the way,
Were content, in the *pass*, to keep thousands at bay,
But these took the *field*, made the onset, with glare
Of torches, each man as a target laid bare !

XXXVI.

Those died where they stood, for their country and laws ;[2]
These triumphed sublimely, for God and his cause ;
Both equal in glory.   The brave can meet death,
But the saints of Jehovah shall triumph by faith.

XXXVII.

O Freedom, thy martyrs are martyrs for God !
And, conquering or dying, the soil they have trod,
In man's last high struggle of body and soul,
Is hallowed while ages on ages shall roll !

XXXVIII.

O Faith, when thy rapture celestial has fired
The souls that Jehovah's own breath has inspired,

[1] At the famous pass of Thermopylæ, when Leonidas and his three hundred fell, resisting Xerxes and his three millions of Persians.

[2] So the beautiful epigrammatic epitaph written for their monument at Thermopylæ by the poet Simonides of Ceos :

'Ω ξεῖν', ἀγγειλον Λακεδαιμονίοις, ὅτι τῇδε
Κείμεθα, τοῖς κείνων πειθόμενοι νομίοις.

which I translate :

Go, Stranger-friend, to glorious Sparta tell
That here, t' obey her laws, we slumber well !

G. L. T.

Then shall one chase a thousand, and two put to flight
Ten thousand fierce foes, in the battle for right !

XXXIX.

God's handful, clean sifted from idols and shirks,
Each soul a burnt offering, faith shown by works,
Stark radicals, stripped of the world, and aflame
With the baptism of fire, shall shake earth in God's name !

XL.

O Church of Jehovah, thy victory know !
'Tis Purity strikes the all-conquering blow ;
And Faith and Devotion, her offspring sublime,
Have conquered for God since the dawning of time.

XLI.

O Zion, o'erwhelmed by the rush of the world,
Thy trumpets all silent, thy banners all furled,
Thy torches unkindled, thy joy and thy shout
All deadened and drowned in an ocean of doubt ;—

XLII.

O Zion, come forth from thy caverns and holes,
And cast thy false gods to the bats and the moles !
Take thy torch and thy trumpet, grasp buckler and sword,
And charge o'er the earth in the might of the Lord !

XLIII.

O Spirit whose breath kindled heroes of old,
And swept the invader in wrath from God's fold,

Rise ! Blow on these ages, and send us once more
The Sword of the Lord and of Gideon of yore !

XLIV.

Then Zion shall shine forth as fair as the moon,
And clear as the sun in the splendor of June !
Like an army with banners shall shout on her way,
And nations be born to the Lord in a day !

XLV.

Then Error's dark legions to night shall be hurled !
Then Zion's pure glory shall gladden the world !
Then the Lord shall descend in his kingdom again,
And Earth shout Hosanna, Heaven echo Amen !

PART II. " FAINT, YET PURSUING."

[Book of Judges, chapter 8.]

I.

" FAINT—faint, yet pursuing," rose Gideon's band,
From Jordan's wild surges to Gilead's land ;
Drenched, battle-worn, weary, they paused not for rest,
For " faint, yet pursuing," is valor's last test.

II.

The "sword of the Lord and of Gideon " had blazed,
A meteor terror, o'er armies amazed,
And Midian and Amalek, swept from their spoil,
In madness and ruin were hurled from God's soil.

III.

Yet full fifteen thousand, escaped from the sword
Through Ephraim's envy, passed armed o'er the ford,
To muster in Karkor the wreck of their state,
And nurse in the desert their vengeance and hate.

IV.

These, too, must be scattered. No power must remain
The war to renew and vex Israel again ;
No moment for glory, or pride's fond deceit,
Till God's work is ended in victory complete.

V.

The chiding of Ephraim's anger is quelled,
The Jordan is forded, with harvest flood swelled ;
Weak, weary, and hungry, from midnight to dawn,
The three hundred heroes through perils press on.

VI.

'Tis sunrise, and Succoth's wide portals unfold,
Where Jacob built booths for his pied herds of old—
"Give bread to your brethren," the victor implored,
"We fight, for your rescue, the wars of the Lord."

VII.

O baseness unspeakable ! Bondage to self !
What cravens and cowards like cowards for pelf ?
"Are Zebah, Zalmunna, thy captives," they whine,
"That we should give bread to these braggarts of thine ?"

VIII.

On, on to Penuel, where Jacob all night
Erst wrestled with God till the dawning of light,
And, gloriously lame, as an "Israel" rose,
A prince with Jehovah, to vanquish his foes.

IX.

Once more the faint call, for what force might demand —
."Give bread, I beseech you, to ration my band ;
We wrestle for God, who here blessed our great sire ;"
But baseness once more stirred the conqueror's ire.

X.

What fitter than scourges of bramble and thorn
For vilest poltroons in man's image e'er born ?
What fitter than overthrow, infamy, shame,
For bosoms that burn not with patriot flame ?

XI.

But vengeance to-morrow—to-day for the foe !
Faint, footsore, and famishing, onward they go,
Through hunger and weariness, sleeplessness, spite,
The taunts of the day, and the gloom of the night.

XII.

From midnight to midnight their iron-like tramp
Rings on, through the blaze of the noon, the chill damp
Of night dews, undaunted by distance or time,
In the grandeur of heroism, stern and sublime !

XIII.

The Jabbok's wild gorge they have threaded at last,
His far-foaming torrent is forded and passed,
And out o'er the desert, beneath the fierce stars,
Sweeps on the swift march by the red light of Mars.

XIV.

Not rash, though relentless, those souls without fear—
The foe will be wary—a watch at his rear ;
Through Nobah and Jogbehah wide their detour,
That smites on the flank his encampment secure.

XV.

Then wild rose the clangor of trumpet and targe !
Then rushed like tornado that lion-like charge !
And Midian's shriek answered Amalek's yell
Where Israel's sword like a thunderbolt fell !

XVI.

One moment of horror, and slaughter, and gore,
And crash, as of shipwreck on hurricane shore,
And, wild o'er the desert, stark, howling, and riven,
That host, like the sand in the whirlwind, is driven.

XVII.

No moment for arming, no refuge, no rest,
By the sword of Jehovah and Gideon pressed,
Till the last wail expires, like a sigh on the blast,
And the brave Baal-fighter is victor at last !

XVIII.

Is Victor ! and Israel, scourged and restored,
Now safely shall dwell in the smile of her Lord ;
While her hero, once scorned, now her sceptre disdains,
And answers—" God only o'er Israel reigns."

XIX.

Ah, " faint, yet pursuing," is valor's last test,
The last pulse of fire in the conqueror's breast ;
Toil, weakness, and treason, and terror outbraved,
The hero endures to the end, and is saved.

XX.

No triumph abides but the triumph o'er all ;
The last foe in armor must fly or must fall ;
Then sweet to the hero is slumber from toil,
In the tents of the vanquished, refreshed with the spoil.

XXI.

O soul in affliction !   O spirit in strife !
In battle for righteousness, liberty, life,
Know, know that all raptures in victory blend,
And, " faint, yet pursuing," pursue to the end !

XXII.

O Thou whose last anguish wrought hope for a world,
And Hell's black invasion to Tartarus hurled,
Gird *us* in all weakness, in peril defend ;
So "faint, yet pursuing," we'll strive to the end.

XXIII.

Then, then, of our Canaan forever possessed,
No foe shall invade our inviolate rest ;
The smile of our Gideon shall sunshine afford,
And peace shall o'erflow in the land of the Lord.

ELISHA'S FIERY CHARIOTS.

[Second Book of Kings, 6: 8–23.]

I.

At Dothan dwelt Elisha, where Joseph's brethren[1] brought
Their herds to fresher pastures, from Shechem's parching
    drought ;
Where, moved with wrathful envy at the seer-like dreams he
    told,
They sold their father's darling for greedy Ishmael's gold.

II.

At Dothan dwelt Elisha, on whom the spirit came
Of great Elijah, snatched to heaven in the chariot of flame ;[2]
And there o'er Israel's welfare he watched with patriot care,
And eyes that farthest saw o'er earth, when closed to earth, in
    prayer.

[1] Gen. 37 : 17.   [2] II. Kings 2 : 11.

III.

Full oft fierce Syria plotted her silent, swift campaign,
But one inspired clairvoyant soul saw every ambush plain ;
Illumed from heaven, clear-seeing, each midnight raid he
    scanned,—
One visioned soul on picket guard, defending all the land ! [1]

IV.

Then Syria's king was troubled, and quaked with nameless
    fear ;
And cried : " Ah, who will show me the traitor lurking here ?"
" No traitor here, but Israel's seer to Israel's king declares
Thy midnight word, thy midnight march, and baffles all thy
    snares."

V.

Then spake Benhadad :[2] " Muster once more a mighty host,
And bring me, captive, Israel's seer, her buckler and her
    boast ;
Who then shall spy our counsels ?—who then, with wizard [3]
    sight,
Shall scan our midnight marches, and foil our conquering
    might ?"

---

[1] Ezek. 3 : 17 and 33 : 7.   [2] II. Kings 6 : 24.

[3] Wizard sight. No doubt this was Benhadad's opinion of the nature of
the inspiration of the Hebrew prophets, making them tricksters, or trance-
seers at best, whose gift was in part natural, in part artificial, and in no
case reliable, or conferring the power of self-defence. This view explains
his attempt to capture Elisha.

VI.

Lo, now, the mighty cordon, by night 'round Dothan drawn,
O'erwhelms her dwellers with amaze, at morning's earliest
  dawn !
Damascus' steel-clad horsemen, her chariots blazing 'round,
An empire marshalled in array, one prophet to confound !

VII.

" Alas ! alas ! my Master !" the trembling servant [1] cries,
" What shall we do ?. How can we 'scape this stern and dire
  surprise ?"
" *They that be for us,*" calmly the dauntless seer replies,
" *Are more than they against us ; Lord, open the young man's eyes.*"

VIII.

One moment from his spirit earth's dimming veil is dashed,—
One moment on his vision the unseen world [2] is flashed !
And lo ! around God's prophet Samaria's mountains flame
With hosts of light whose cohorts bright no mortal tongue
  can name !

IX.

Legion on legion ! Phalanx on phalanx ! Square on square !
In dense and serried splendor they garrison [3] the air !

---

[1] Not Gehazi, who had been smitten with leprosy and dismissed (II. Kings
5 : 27), but probably some young prophet from the schools, who had not
yet seen the wonders of a full inspiration.
  [2] " Millions of spiritual creatures walk the earth
   Unseen, both when we wake and when we sleep."
  [3] Psa. 34 : 7.   —" Paradise Lost," iv., 676 ; also Heb. 1 : 14.

And steeds of dazzling brightness, and chariots all ablaze
With ruby fire, where emerald tire round diamond axle plays !

X.

One moment on the mortal the heavenly vision glowed,—
One chariot for Elijah,[1] to waft his soul to God,—
But thousands ! myriads ! millions ! in unseen hosts sublime.[2]
To fight Jehovah's battles here upon the fields of time !

XI.

And when God's saints illumined by faith that lights the mind,
Behold his power, and joy in him, then all their foes are blind ;
Like humbled Syria's legions, an army captive led
By that one swordless man they marched to take, alive or
    dead !

XII.

O Soul, know thou thy convoy through all this low dark life,
Amid its toils and sorrows, its bitterness and strife ;
The bright " heaven lies about us " not " in infancy "[3] alone,—
Heaven bathes and swathes this living world through every
    age and zone.

XIII.

And he who, rapt and lifted, illumed by light divine,
In God, for God, obeys, shall see that viewless world outshine ;
All eye, all ear, all spiritual sense, the spiritual world shall ken,
And know his own apocalypse, and walk a seer 'mongst men.

---

[1] II. Kings 2 : 11.   [2] Psa. 68 : 17 ; Hab. 3 : 8 ; Zech. 6 : 1-7.
[3] " Heaven lies about us in our infancy."
    —*Wordsworth*, " Intimations of Immortality," v. 9.

XIV.

And he who, 'gainst ten thousand embattled for the wrong,
Still meekly, boldly stands for God, in God's strength only
    strong,—
For him God's re-enforcements omnipotent shall ride ;
Rivers and stars [1] and unknown worlds shall battle on his side.

XV.

Stand then, O Soul, serenely, God's sentry in thy place,
In instant prayer, with opened eyes, and speak thy word, by
    grace ;
And he who would o'erwhelm thee, by guile or tyrant rod,
Must meet the universe in arms, and measure swords with
    God.

———————

JEHOSHAPHAT'S DELIVERANCE.

[Second Book of Chronicles, chapter 20 ; and Joel, chapter 3.]

I.

JEHOSHAPHAT reigned over Judah in peace ;
The land lay in quiet and teemed with increase ;
For righteousness ruled, from the cot to the throne,
And Judah rejoiced in Jehovah alone.

II.

For (Baal's base worship once hurled from God's land)
Prosperity poured from his liberal hand ;
The law was revered and the temple restored,
And Salem shone bright in the smile of her Lord.

[1] Kishon and the " stars in their courses."—JUDGES 5 : 20, 21.

III.

Then came a swift message of terror and fear :
" Lo, Moab, and Ammon, and Edom from Seir,
Have swarmed from the desert, a numberless host,
To pillage our cities and plunder our coast !

IV.

"From Moab's black mount, down the Scorpion-pass,
They have marched by the sea-shore, a myriad mass ;
And now on their rapine already they gloat,
In the Forest of Palms, by the Fount of the Goat !

V.

" A black cloud of evil, a whirlwind of fate,
One day's rapid march from Jerusalem's gate ;
Like locusts they light upon Judah's fair realm !
Like demons descend to devour and o'erwhelm !"

VI.

Then trembling Jehoshaphat feared and proclaimed
A fast for all Judah ; and sacrifice flamed,
And Judah's strong warriors, with children, and wives,
In the house of Jehovah implored for their lives.

VII.

" Lord God of our fathers, in heaven adored,
Thou rulest on earth, our Omnipotent Lord ;
Fierce kingdoms of heathen obey thy command ; ·
The might of thy majesty none can withstand !

VIII.

" Art thou not our God, who hast sworn to defend
Forever the children of Abrah'm thy friend ?
Who gav'st us this land, and forbad'st us to slay
Our fierce, jealous kindred, who'd make us their prey ?

IX.

" Behold in thy presence our little ones stand,
Like lambs in thy fold when the wolf is at hand !
O wilt thou not judge them ? thy terror we know ;
Thy might to o'erwhelm our implacable foe !

X.

" No might of our own, no prowess we boast
To meet and to vanquish this numberless host,
Nor know we aught farther ; our eyes are on thine ;"—
The verge of the human *must* touch the divine !

XI.

Then swift on the singer Jahaziel came
The Spirit of God, like a baptism of flame.
From the midst of the people, who prostrate adored,
He leapt, as on fire with the word of the Lord !

XII.

" Ho ! Hearken all Judah ! Jerusalem sad,
And thou, King Jehoshaphat, hear and be glad !
For thus saith Jehovah, your champion divine :
' Ye bring me your battle—I take it as mine !

XIII.

" 'To-morrow go down ; yet ye go not to fight,
But to stand and behold my salvation and might ;
To shout, while Jehovah shall charge on the foe,
With nameless and awful and utter o'erthrow ! ' "

XIV.

Then prostrate, adoring, fell monarch and throng ;
Then thundered, exultant, the Kohathite song ;
And cymbal and psaltery, timbrel and lyre,
Awoke at the rapture and wafted it higher.

XV.

Then bold on the morrow, unawed, undismayed,
Marched forth to God's battle that weird cavalcade ;
Unarmed and unarmored, no shield and no sword,
Sole trusting the terrible word of the Lord.

XVI.

Tekoa's wild echoes their anthems rebound,
And Jéruel's wilderness wakes at the sound ;
Not war songs of slaughter, not wrath at the foe,
But the Beauty of Holiness swells as they go.

XVII.

The mercies of God that forever endure,
His judgments tremendous, his righteousness sure,
His kindness unchanging, his goodness untold,
With song and with trumpet the grand pæan rolled !

XVIII.

Then lo! as unconsciously onward they trod,
Leapt forth on their foe the dread ambush of God!
The power that breathes order, and star-clusters burn,
Bade chaos and madness one moment return!

XIX.

For Moab and Ammon and Maon and Seir,
In anger and jealousy, frenzy and fear,
Have rent the fierce compact which now they abhor,
And charged on each other, like whirlwinds at war!

XX.

And Moab and Ammon on Edom now wheel;
And Maon is swept with their tempest of steel;
Then, frantic, they rush on each other in ire,
And all in a whirlpool of slaughter expire!

XXI.

What wizard his wand of enchantment has waved?
What demon his dire malediction has raved?
What magic infernal, no numbers can name,
Has hurled on whole armies its mind-scorching flame?

XXII.

'Tis the arm of Jehovah, for Zion made bare!
'Tis his banner of wrath blazing out on the air!
'Tis the scath of his vengeance, the blast of his breath,
Sweeping hot as the fire-wind o'er harvests of death!

XXIII.

'Tis a heaven-sent fury God's foes to confound !
'Tis his meteor sword dealing madness around !
Till the last fierce invader lies pale and o'erthrown
Where red heaps of havoc and slaughter are strewn !

XXIV.

Then, from her high watch-tower, afar o'er the plain,
Gazed Judah in awe over myriads slain,
And heaped a new harvest from blood-watered soil ;
Of jewels and trappings and raiment and spoil.

XXV.

Three days swelled that harvest of treasure untold,
A harvest unplanted, a trophy of gold,
Till the storm that descended in wrath to destroy
Left Judah exulting in riches and joy.

XXVI.

Then blessings untold from Berachah ascend ;
Then trumpet and cornet and cithara blend
With tabret and dulcimer, sackbut and shalm,
In Zion's Hosanna, her rapturous psalm.

XXVII.

And Judah, delivered, through time shall declare
The power all-victorious of penitent prayer—
The prayer that falls prostrate on promises strong,
Till flashes God's answer in fire and in song.

XXVIII.

And nations are awed at Jehovah's dread might,
Whose arm overwhelming fought Israel's fight ;
And ages his "rest round about" [1] shall record,
Who dared leave his battle alone to the Lord.

XXIX.

And prophets shall sing, until prophecy fail,
The judgment of God in Jehoshaphat's vale ; [2]
Dread vale of Decision !—where nations shall crowd
To the doom of the world, from Christ's throne on the cloud !

XXX.

Then, then shall Jehovah earth's mighty bring low, [3]
Her winepress be full, and her vats overflow ; [4]
Then sinners like chaff from God's flail [5] shall be driven,
But Judah, his saints, shall be garnered in heaven.

---

[1] II. Chron. 20 : 30.

[2] Joel 3 : 2.   The name Jehoshaphat means "Judgment of Jehovah."   An old Jewish tradition makes the scene of this victory to be the appointed place of the world's final judgment.

[3] Ibid. 3 : 12—*margin.*

[4] Ibid. 3 : 13.   Treading the winepress is a symbol of retribution.

[5] Ibid. 3 : 14.   "Valley of Decision," *margin* of A. V. " *Concision* or *threshing,*" which is the judgment and separation of the wheat and the chaff.

THE FIERY FURNACE.

[Book of Daniel, chapter 3, and Song of the Three Holy Children.]

I.

WHAT means this mighty concourse on Dura's boundless plain;
The trumpet's peal, the clang of steel, till earth resounds
    again ?
Old Babylon has opened her hundred gates of brass,
Through every arch her cohorts march, her hundred armies
    pass.

II.

Still swells the matchless muster, with banners far unfurled,
O'er barbarous hosts from far-off coasts that bound the Asian
    world ;
And provinces and kingdoms and cities in array,
With princes, captains, rulers, join to honor this great day.

III.

Great Nebuchadnezzar's empire in splendor girds his throne
Where he, in godlike majesty, sits dazzling and alone ;
This day shall crown his triumphs, this day shall swell his
    fame,
And spread through all the orient world the glory of his
    name.

IV.

There towers the votive statue, the gift of spoils untold,
Colossal grandeur in its form, and all refulgent gold ;
To mighty Bel, the conqueror's god, his homage proud is
     shown,
But king and god are one, for lo ! the features are his own !

V.

Then sounds the proclamation, by herald's trumpets flung
Afar o'er all the countless throng in many a various tongue :—
" What time the sound of cornet and flute and harp shall rise,
And sackbut, psaltery, dulcimer, shall mingle in the skies,—

VI.

" Then every tribe and nation in reverent worship fall,
And own the god set up by him whose sceptre rules ye all ;
And he who falls not prostrate yon fiery furnace claims,—
For him awaits the instant doom of yon devouring flames !"

VII.

Thus runs the tyrant's mandate.   Anon sweet strains ascend,
And billowy waves of harmony with all the breezes blend ;
And now the abject myriads, far as the anthems sound,
With mitred priests and sceptred kings, fall grovelling on
     the ground !

VIII.

Not all ! Three youthful rulers, with forms of Hebrew mould,
Hard by the throne itself, bow not, but stand erect and bold ;

'Mid mightiest peers, and pontiffs dread, unawed they stand
    serene,
Nor bow the head, nor droop the eye, nor change their stead-
    fast mien.

IX.

In wrath then spake the monarch : " My gods dare ye despise ?
And flout my summons thus before an empire's gazing eyes ?
Perchance ye erred,—I know your worth ! When next the
    anthems swell
Bow down, I'll pardon your rash youth ; so all shall yet be
    well.

X.

" But if ye bow not prostrate, nor own my gods ordained,
In yonder blazing furnace I'll cast ye, bound and chained ;
Then what god of the nations shall save you from my hand ?
Be warned ! Trust not to Him ye served in Judah's conquered
    land !"

XI.

Then calm, and clear, and dauntless, outspake the youthful
    three :
" Most gracious Liege, we need no thought to frame our word
    for thee ;
If such our lot that 'mid yon flames we be this moment cast,
Our God can save, if such his will ; we'll trust him to the last.

XII.

" If not his will to save us, e'en so his will is good ;
But know, O king, that saved or burned, we will not serve
    thy god ;

Thy honors past with thanks we own, with thanks, too, we
resign ;
Life's supreme hour mocks earthly power ; here we are God's,
not thine !"

XIII.

Then red with speechless fury the tyrant's visage burned,
And from the faithful three his face—the seal of doom—he
turned !
" Ho ! Heat yon furnace hotter seven times than e'er before !"
'Tis done, till bursting to the sky the mad flames belch and
roar !

XIV.

" Ho ! bring the mightiest of my host, this brazen three to
bind,
And hurl them where the scorching flames shall tame their
towering mind !
Braved to my face ! So realms shall learn to tremble at my
nod,
Nor fools invoke that vengeful stroke that brooks nor man nor
god !"

XV.

So raved the worm ! His mightiest lords obey the sentence
dire,
The unresisting three fall bound amid the torrid fire !
So fierce the flame its instant scath th' unwilling sheriffs slew;
When lo ! astonishment o'erspread the monarch's face to
view !

XVI.

Up from his throne in haste he sprang, with fixed and awestruck gaze,

"Did we not cast *three* men, in chains, 'mid yon devouring
blaze ?

But lo! *four* forms walk loose, unhurt, as though at ease
they trod

The powerless flames, and that fourth form shines glorious
as a god !"

XVII.

For there amid the raging heat God's Covenant Angel came,

And from the oven's roaring vault smote out the blasting
flame ;

And now a cool and whistling wind like evening round them
plays,

While wide around their songs resound, their shouts of joy
and praise !

XVIII.

No more the monarch's pride rebels, nor mightiest lords he
sends ;

On royal feet, with footsteps fleet, in gladness he descends ;

Before the furnace's mouth he stands, while wondering nations
see :—

"Ho ! ye who serve the Lord Most High, come forth, and
come to me !"

XIX.

Now forth from out those roaring flames God's joyful servants come,

With heavenly grace on every face, while earth and hell stand
    dumb !
And princes, pontiffs, potentates, the jury of the world,
Attest them scathless ! Not a hair is singed, a vestment
    curled !

XX.

Then cried the conquered conqueror, with hands to heav'n
    upraised :—
" The God of Shadrach, Meshach, and Abed-nego be praised !
Who saved his saints who trusted him, and dared their king
    defy,
That they might serve their God alone, for him might live, or
    die !

XXI.

" Hear now, ye nations, our decree. We own, till life shall
    end,
The God of Shadrach, Meshach, and Abed-nego, our Friend.
His holy name let none blaspheme, but all his power revere ;
That God can save beyond the grave, who thus can rescue
    here."

XXII.

Then mighty Babylon rejoiced, and hailed the glorious
    band
Who braved for right an empire's might, and changed the
    king's command ;
And royal favor crowned their worth, and wealth, and length
    of days ;
For honors won by right well done both men and angels praise.

XXIII.

Lord, when we stand, at thy command, to face earth's wrath
    or shame,
To dare its dangerous flatteries, or persecuting flame,
Alike in all on thee we'll call for grace this truth to spy :—
When life is death, then death is life, and blest are they who die!

THE SCOURGING OF HELIODORUS.

[Second Book of Maccabees, chapter 3.]

I.

THE Grecian kings of Syria, the proud Seleucid stock,
Filled Alexander's Asian throne in glorious Antioch ;
From Hellas's isles to India's streams their banners, wide
    unfurled,
From Scythian wastes to Persian seas, waved o'er the Orient
    world.

II.

And Palestina, subject long beneath their conquering sway,
Though ravaged oft, now throve in peace through many a
    prosperous day,
While good Onias, wise and just, ruled in Jerusalem,
Where Aaron's mitre long survived great David's diadem.

III.

There mighty Cyrus, far revered, a name almost divine,
Inspired by Heaven had reared once more Jehovah's hallowed
    shrine ;

And Gentile kings from far-off lands had crowned that holy
    fane
With gifts untold, and there asked peace and blessings on their
    reign.

IV.

All tributes paid, still gifts o'erflowed ; and sumless treasures
    rare,
The wealth of merchants, princes, realms, sought sanctuary
    there ;
The maiden's dower, the orphan's share, the widow's portion
    sure,
There slept inviolate, with tithes that fed the nation's poor.

V.

But graceless Simon, sworn to guard that treasury divine,
'Gainst just Onias stirred with rage and envy most malign,
To heathen foes that trust betrayed, in infamy untold,
And moved the Syrian tyrant's greed to grasp the hallowed
    gold.

VI.

Then King Seleucus sent with guile the warder of his
    hoard,
Bold Heliodorus, charged to rob the temple of the Lord :
Through Cœlosyria's subject towns, Phœnicia's conquered
    powers,
In well-feigned state he strays, then speeds to Zion's holy
    towers.

VII.

Ah, who can tell what pall-like woe hung Salem's city o'er,
As Heliodorus' dire demand was told from door to door !
From street to street a doleful cry of anguish rent the air—
Ten thousand stretched their hands to heaven, ten thousand
      bowed in prayer.

VIII.

Fair women, girt with sackcloth harsh beneath their tender
      breasts,
Wailed through the town, and virgins moaned, and tore their
      snowy vests ;
The full-robed Levites, prostrate low, before God's altar
      lay,
And cried : " Jehovah, guard thine own ! Defend thy cause
      this day !"

IX.

But ah, that good and great high-priest ! 'Twas fearful to
      behold
What speechless agony of prayer his ghastly visage told !
What grief, what shame, for orphans robbed, for God's pure
      shrine profaned—
Yet on his mournful, awful face a startling brightness reigned !

X.

But Heliodorus, eager, rash, that ruthless mandate urged,
And trod Jehovah's hallowed courts in Gentile guilt, un-
      purged ;
His bandit guard around him stood, the sacrilege began,

When lo ! God's instant glory blazed, to whelm the pride of
    man !

XI.

Forth rushed, caparisoned most fair, a steed of dazzling
    mould,
Who bore a rider terrible, complete in harnessed gold !
And fierce with hoofs all shod with fire he smote the impious
    foe ;
His breath was flame ! His eyes like coals ! His mane a
    meteor's glow !

XII.

And two celestial youths stood there, in robes of lustrous white,
Glorious in beauty, excellent in majesty and might.
And swift with rods of baleful gleam, while quaking Antioch
    saw,
They scourged, with sore and vengeful strokes, the scorner of
    God's law !

XIII.

Down Heliodorus fell, amain, in dark and deathlike swoon,
As fell proud Saul, when Christ from heaven outflashed the
    summer noon !
Fainting with awe they bore him forth from that thrice dire-
    ful place.
Then flew to God's high-priest to crave incensed Jehovah's
    grace.

XIV.

The dread saint prays—the Gentile lives, and hies him to his
    lord ;

He tells the glorious power of Him on Zion's height adored ;

The king, enraged, asks : "Whom, once more, whom braver, shall I send ?"

" Thy foes, O king," the stern reply, "their madness thus shall end !"

XV.

Ah, ye who grasp at others' wealth, nor dread Heaven's righteous wrath ;

Whose hordes, like locust bands, devour the poor with wasting scath ;

Who rule for gain, whose law is self, whose god is sordid gold ;

Whose sway is outrage legalized ; shame, conscience, manhood sold ;

XVI.

Woe ! woe ! to all your pirate crew ! Wolves, vultures of your race !

Plagues, pests, and vermin of mankind, whate'er your pride and place ;

Be warned ! Beware ! crime's longest day must end, and judgment come ;

Haste ! Justice whets th' avenging sword, and Mercy's lips grow dumb !

THE WORLD-WIDE [1] HOPE.

"WILL it be morning soon ?"— the world is sad ;
When will the morning come, and make it glad?—
"Will it be morning soon ?" ask hearts that pray,
And toil, and wait, for some great, brighter day ;—
"Will it be morning soon ?" the ages cry,
As, one by one, earth's eras wander by ;—
"When will the earth-night break, the heaven-sun shine,
With dawn, and day, and deep, full noon, divine ?"—

"Will it be morning soon ?" O, soul of man ;
Since the sad flight of long, long years began,
How oft, how echoless, that nameless prayer
Has wandered, voiceless, on the waste of air,
While hearts, rich fraught with longing, waiting trust,
Sank cold to silence, and grew still in dust !

"Will it be morning soon ?" Since that sad night
Whose shadow fell on Eden's rosy light ;
When Sin bore Death and Sorrow at one birth—

[1] The title of this poem is designed to express that universal expectation of a coming Deliverer and a future better age, in this or some other state of existence, which is found in all the prominent religious systems of the Gentile world, and which is no doubt a traditionary remnant of the Eden record and of the great Eden promise of Genesis 3 : 15.

The death of purity, and blight of earth ;
The dear, dear memories of that primal morn
Have hung, like angels, o'er the race forlorn ;
And vague bright dreams of rapture yet to be,
Like sunbeams trembling down the sunless sea,
Have gleamed, prophetic of that longed-for time,
On gifted souls of every age and clime.

'Tis the great hope of all the general race,
Unchilled through time. uncircumscribed by space ;
Confused, yet vital, through all creeds and songs,
The vision of all teachings, times, and tongues.

The child of Brahma[1] mourns, by Gunga's[2] wave,
That Brahma comes not to avenge and save :
Three thousand years too long has Brahma stayed ;
The Vedas void, the Shastras all gainsaid ;
Greek, Roman, Tartar, Mongol, Briton, spoil,
Age after age, earth's oldest, brightest soil ;
Yet Brahma lingers in some sphere above,
Creating, warring, or dissolved in love ;
Changeless through forms innumerous, conquering flies,
Forgets the world, and revels round the skies.

[1] In the Brahminical system—the older portions of which form without doubt the oldest systematic Gentile religion now extant—there have been numerous avatars or incarnations of Brahma, and another is yet expected, in which wrong and evil are to be banished from the world, and eternal blessedness is to begin. Material for reference is too abundant to need mention.

[2] Gunga, the sacred river Ganges, personified as a goddess.

The Buddhist [1] seer, from Sakyamuni's line,
Still fondly dreams Gautama was divine ;
Longs for the far-off time that brings once more
Incarnate Boodh, to ransom and restore ;
And toils with studious, life-long, watchful woes,
To earn Nirvana's passionless repose,
Where transmigration with existence ends,
And each Enlightened soul with Buddha blends.

Prometheus,[2] bound, still braves the wrath of Jove,
And bleeds for man, with death-defying love ;
Derides the Thunderer's ineffective rage,
And saves mankind for some propitious age ;
An age that swept, prophetic, on the soul
Of him whose virtues won the Hemlock [3] bowl,

---

[1] The Buddhist system was a revolt, a heresy, or originally a reform, from Brahminism. It was originated at Kapilāvastu, near the sacred city of Benares, between five and six hundred years before Christ, by the Prince Siddartha, who became the last incarnation of Buddha. He was the son of Suddhodana, the Rajah of Kapilavastu, of the Sakya clan (whence his title Sakyamuni), a branch of the great Gautama stock, whence his name Gautama is the great eponymic surname of his race. He died at Kusingara, in the kingdom of Oudh, B.C. 543, aged eighty years. Nirvana is the Boodhist heaven, an actionless and passionless existence, of merely negative attributes, so closely akin in conception to non-existence as to amount practically to atheism and annihilation. See cyclopædias and special treatises, especially Otto and Ristner's "Buddha and his Doctrines," Trübner & Co., London, 1869. The canonical books of southern Buddhism are about twice the volume of the Bible.

[2] The Prometheus legend is one of the most beautiful of the classical polytheism, and one of the most important, theologically, as being the one most clearly representing the Messianic tradition in its classical form. See Keightley's Mythology, classical dictionaries, and cyclopædias.

[3] Socrates, who was condemned to drink the Hemlock.

And winged the Attic bird [1] to heights sublime,
That still o'ertop the toiling march of time.

Scandinia's Skalds [2] erst sang the woe-fraught hour
When Baldur fell, by Lokè's baneful power ;
When virtue died, and Woden, Freia, Thor,—
Valhalla's gods of wassail and of war—
Usurped the world. But, though Yggdrasil's height
Towers through three heavens, and waves in utmost light,
A shattering shock shall blight its shuddering shade,
Its fountains fail, its flowery foliage fade ;
Existence, wrecked, resolve in misty floods,
And chaos reign, the Twilight of the gods.
Then shall the saga's mystic lore be plain,
And Baldur live, and build the world again ;
Sin be no more, and good men, snatched from night,
With Baldur dwell in Gimlè's golden light.

[1] " The olive grove of Academe,
Plato's retirement, where the Attic bird
Trills her thick-warbled notes the summer long."
—*Milton*, " Paradise Regained," Bk. iv., line 244.

[2] In the Scandinavian or Gothic-Teutonic mythology, Baldur, the god of good, is slain by Lokè, the god of evil, and the Valhalla gods come in. But they are to be overthrown ; the great ash tree of existence, the living universe, Yggdrasil, is to wither and perish ; and gods and men with it. Then Baldur is to have a resurrection, and the universe is to be restored as an eternal heaven. This is another of the most striking of all Gentile forms of the Eden and Messianic traditions combined, symbolizing the fall and moral decay of man effected by evil powers, and his redemption, the new creation, and eternal blessedness. But it confounds the fall of man with the death of the redeemer for man, in the death of Baldur.

The Shaman [1] faith, that rules the Arctic land
From Norway's cape to Behring's far-off strand,—
That first the mighty Mongol's flag unfurled,
And hurled tremendous Jenghis on the world,—
Still waits for Radien's coming, swift and bright,
From softer seas whence springs the boreal light,
To stretch the sceptre of his cheering reign
From Bothnia's streams, o'er all the Tundra plain,
And bring the transient, wandering sun, to pour
On bleak Siberia summer, evermore.

The nomad Tartar [2] waits for Heaven's great Khan
To purge the world, and right the wrongs of man ;
Beholds his comet steeds that sweep the sky
With manes of fire, to bring deliverance nigh ;
And dreams on Gobi's waste and boundless sands,
Of that great oasis, Eden of all lands,

[1] Shamanism, the religion of all the Pagan Mongol and Tartar tribes of northern Asia, is one of the oldest primitive Pagan religions of the world, a nature-worship and devil-worship, yet having the great monotheistic conception lying inert at its base, with a prophecy that a great and beneficent spirit shall one day come to deliver the world from the dominion of the demons men are now compelled to worship. He is to appear from the north, on the beams of the aurora borealis, and bring with him the warmer climate, in search of which Arctic animal life migrates northward in winter.

[2] The non-Mongol Tartar religions lose the Arctic ideas and assume those of the desert steppe and oasis, with a strong tinge from Lamaïsm, which is the paganized form of Boodhism, as Romanism is the paganized form of Christianity. Naturally to the desert life of the Tartar the horse (which was probably there first domesticated) is the sacred animal, instead of the cow, as in India, and the horse-flesh feast, as among the ancient Scandinavians (who were probably of the same race), is their highest religious ceremony.

Once by glad feet of sinless mortals trod,
When time was young, and earth was near to God.

Tezcuco's [1] altar, like th' Athenians', stood
Sacred to one all-causing, Unknown God,
Whose monarch-bard in song's sweet numbers told
What bright revolving ages should unfold,
When Mexic's clime should know and bless the reign
Of Him the visioned prophet sought in vain.

Cholula [2] mourned when Quetzalcoatl divine,
Beloved, but wronged, forsook his conquered shrine ;

[1] Tezcuco, the capital of the Acolhua nation, was the centre of a peaceful and highly cultured civilization and religion in the Valley of Anahuac, before the founding of Mexico there by the savage, conquering Aztecs in A.D. 1325. Its poet-king, Nezhualcoyotl, built a nine-storied temple, with a starry roof representing the firmament, in honor of the invisible deity called Tloquenahuaque, " he who is all in himself," or Ipalnemoan, " he by whom we live," expressions of infinity and self-existence foreign to the Pagan world, and surprisingly like true revelation. In this temple, and in the system of religion to which it belonged, the horrible human sacrifices of the Aztecs were unknown. The worship consisted of songs, prayers, incense, and flowers. This form of religion was, however, little known to the masses of the people, and bears marks of having been a missionary religion from the Old World, and probably descended from the patriarchal religion of the Old Testament, perhaps from Christianity itself. (For this and the following note see Bancroft's " Native Races," etc., Tylor's " Anahuac or Mexico," and Cyc. Brit., ninth edition, article Mexico.)

[2] Cholula was the centre of another Mexican religion, probably more ancient than that of Tezcuco, and founded by that mysterious personage, Quetzalcoatl, who was undoubtedly a deified white missionary from Europe. He was taller than the natives (as the whites are), with white skin, European features, hair and long beard, both black (the natives are brown and beardless), long flowing robes, and came among them from a foreign country, to which

Left the bright Anahuac he could not save,
And launched, lamented, o'er th' Atlantic wave.
Birds, breezes, blossoms, drooped for Aztec Pan,
And maize fields sighed soft sympathy with man.
Long grew the ages, but his pledged return
The Aztec saw where morn's bright splendors burn,
And hailed his advent when the Spaniard came—
But found his god a fiend of blood and flame !

Once Hiawatha[1] came, but comes no more,
From far Superior's pictured, sunset shore,
To teach the hunter how to bend his bow,
The angler where the sturgeon waits below ;
To clear the streams, to tame the savage wild,
And train to peacful arts the forest's child.

he returned by the Atlantic Ocean. He appeared among the Toltec nation, the first and most highly civilized and most important of all the Nahua peoples. They probably excelled in the arts every nation in Europe except Moorish Spain and Italy in the ages in which they lived. He spent twenty years teaching them peace and virtue, a mild religion with only bread, flowers, and perfumes for its sacrifices, and also picture writing, the calendar, and silver-smithing, which long flourished at Cholula, the Toltec capital. When he departed he told the Cholulans that in future ages his brethren, white and bearded men like himself, should come from over the sea, where the sun rises, and rule their country. The great pyramid of Cholula, with its hemispherical temple of Quetzalcoatl on the summit, was twice as long and high as the great teoclli of the sun at Mexico, and many ages must have elapsed to bring it, in that dry climate, to its present state of ruin.

[1] The Hiawatha myth among the American Indians needs no other commentary than Longfellow's poem upon it ; or rather than what the poem might and would have been, had its scholarly and genial author selected a stronger and more commanding form of versification for the finest Indian legend of America.

What means this golden, universal dream,
Dower of the world ?—Comes there no radiant beam
From brighter spheres, through prophet, bard, or sage,
To explain this world-hope of some happier age ?

'Tis Heaven's great promise, written on the race,
That man shall yet regain his primal place !
Some great uplifting, yet, earth's years must bring,
Or hope is vain, and faith a fruitless thing.
Man, universal, feels and mourns his fall,
His blight, his ruin, though he knows not all ;
But from the garden and the ark he bore
Heaven's pledge and promise to earth's wildest shore :
Though dark its purport, and obscurer grown,
Perplexed, distorted, shadowy, and unknown,
Mixed with strange dreams, and monstrous rites abhorred,
So all unlike Heaven's holy, loving Lord,
Yet, sires to sons, and seers, and minstrels hoar,
Still told, and saw, and sung, the mystic lore,
And Hope, in doubt, like a blind angel lost,
Through error's chaos groped for Heaven's bright coast.

Will it be morning, soon ?   O sage ! O seer !
O Watchman !   Tell us is the morning near ?
Our hearts grew weary with the long, long night,
And break with sighing for the sweet, sweet light !
O watchers on the mountain-tops of time,
Where all the hopes of all the ages climb,

Say if not 'round those heavenward summits play
The purpling tints of near and hastening day ?

Will it be morning, soon ?   What means this stir,
Like that which wakes some giant slumberer,
A slow and gradual rousing, strong and deep,
As the great world shakes off its time-long sleep !

'Tis God's almighty, all-awakening voice,
That bids the race look upward and rejoice !
Startling the nations with its quickening call,
It swells and deepens 'round this echoing ball,
Flies on all winds, and loads with every breeze,
The multitudinous thunder of the seas,
And fills the world's great dithyramb sublime,
Like the grand march of long, resounding rhyme.

The world is waking !   Eighteen hundred years
Roll back in vista, and the hour appears
When down the dimness of earth's gloom forlorn,
From opening skies, broke in the first, clear morn ;
And though ten centuries swept, in cloudy night,
Between men's eyes, and that long-looked-for light,
The sun still shone, and when his mounting ray
Dissolved the shadows ; lo, the night was day !

Will it be morning soon ?   O, waiting race,
Take heart !   Look up !   The darkness flies apace !
The blood-red dawn, with fagot, sword and flame,
Faded, as sunrise near and nearer came ;

The morn is here ! Truth's sun rides warm and high,
In kindling splendor, up the opening sky ;
Bright from that burning sphere, with broadening beams,
Light flows and flashes in a thousand streams,
And glad-eyed angels, in man's bliss to share,
Bend in bright ranks from all the hymnful air.

Up ! Brothers, up ! Earth's twilight dreams are done.
And Truth's great, final work-day is begun !
Up ! Brothers, up ! and join the glorious strife,
Where man is struggling toward a loftier life !
Deep through earth's yearning, universal heart,
New hopes, new energies, new being start ;
Old bondage breaks, old chains are rent and riven,
Freedom from all her mountains shouts to Heaven ;
False creeds are crumbling ; man's first faith and best,
The source of all the good in all the rest,
The pure, the bright, the heavenly, and the true,
Eternal, vital, and for ever new,
This, this, instinct with impulse from above,
Goes conquering on, to rule the world by love !

Up ! Brothers, up ! and in this glad employ,
Go forth for God, and sow the world with joy !
Wind of the Spirit blow o'er every land !
Sea of the glory break on every strand !
Hope of the ages, haste all climes to cheer !
Hearts of the nations ; lo, THE MORN IS HERE !

THE INCARNATION.

PART FIRST. A CHRISTMAS CAROL.

[Luke, chapter 2.]

I.

THE EXPECTATION.

A SPELL lay on the world.   The time had come,
By Judah's seers and bards so long foretold,
When that mysterious promise, whereon hung
The endless destiny of all man's race—
First made in Eden, that the woman's seed
Should bruise the serpent's head—must be fulfilled.
Four thousand times and more this spinning globe
Had wheeled her measured circuit through the sky,
And on her latest compass now drew near,
With joyful speed, to the momentous goal.
  Tradition, from old time, with mystic awe
Had spread her Eden-lore through every clime,
Blent with vain dreams, by demon rites profaned,
Perverted, yet portending good to man.
The dusky Hindu looked for Brahma's wheels
Once more to flame in India's sunset sky,
Restoring earth, her rounded cycles filled.
The roving Tartar, on his boundless plains,

Watched for the Khan of Heaven, whose comet steeds,
With manes of fire, should sweep a conquered world.
The Persian Magi saw, with thoughtful joy,
The constellations shaped to aspects new,
That omened undiscovered bliss to earth.
The Sibyl, blinking from her cave, beheld
Strange gods and heard strange mutterings underground,
That oracled Judea's conquering Lord.
All Syria looked, expectant, for a hand
From Salem stretched, to grasp earth's eldest crowns
And blend the world's wide empires into one ;
And seer-like souls caught the deep throb that thrilled
Through silent centuries on that conscious time.
Dire Janus closed his gates ; some mystic power,
In every tribe and realm, unfelt before,
Whispered through all the world, and called for peace ;
Till earth her wars and discords laid aside,
And meekly waited for her coming Lord.
The era is complete, the epoch dawns,
And through the dusk of prophecy broad beams,
Effulgent kindling, speak earth's morning nigh.

II.

THE PREPARATION.

THE Shiloh, long delayed, draws near ;
  For Zion's sacred seers of old
Have shown where soon he shall appear,
  And Bethlehem is the spot foretold—

The seat of David's royal line,
Complete in David's heir divine.

Now Rome's wide sceptre swayed the earth,
  And tribute claimed from every land.
Peoples and tribes of various birth
  Were marshalled at her great command :
So Heaven's deep plan, through world-wide powers,
Brings David's seed to Bethlehem's towers.

Lo ! now, what bands of pilgrims wend
  O'er many a road their toilsome way ?
Toward Ephrath's gates all footsteps tend,
  As sunset gilds fate's final day ;
And golden beams, through gates of even,
Bathe domes and towers in hues of Heaven.

Amid the gathering thousands now,
  Behold a pair of humble mien.
No badge of royal race they show,
  Amid the throng they pass unseen.
No room for them the inn can spare,
The rich, the proud, the gay are there.

The cavern stall is all the place
  That shelters from the chill of night
The maid, most honored of her race,
  In woman's weakest, proudest plight,
The virgin wife, who ere next morn
Crowns earth with God, as mortal born.

The patient oxen eye her couch
  With strange brute instinct's homage, dim ;
The toiling asses silent crouch,
  Nor mar the lowly vesper-hymn
Which floats to heaven, one trembling strain,
As slumber falls o'er town and plain.

III.

THE INCARNATION.

Lo ! while earth in silence lies,
Ope the portals of the skies !
Down the dusk of midnight glooms
Sounds the sweep of myriad plumes !
Shining cohorts, mailed in gold,
Round that cave their vigil hold.

Rank on rank, the squadrons bright
Wheel and form in squares of light.
Grandest names on heaven's old guard
Here to-night keep watch and ward ;
Lean o'er diamond blades, on wings ;
Reverent wait the King of kings.

Tenderest hands that heaven can lend
By yon glimmering lamp attend ;
Watch the anxious hours away
Round that couch of fragrant hay ;
Swift with ministries divine,
Sister spirits wait the sign.

Hark ! A new-born infant's cry
Thrills through hell, and earth, and sky !
Hark ! the clash of shield and sword !
Hark ! the shout that hails him Lord !
Lord of earth, and hell, and heaven !
God in man, to mortals given !

IV.

THE CELEBRATION.

Hail moment blest !   All hail, thou Prince and Saviour !
  Infant Redeemer !   Everlasting King !
On earth good-will toward man, and peace and favor,
  Shout heaven and earth, and let the echo ring !
    Glory ! Glory ! Glory ! Glory !
    Seraphs catch the joyful story !
    Where the silent midnight reigns
    Over Judah's peaceful plains,
      And shepherds watch with pride
      Their warm flocks slumbering wide,
        With rapturous speed they fly.
        First one alone draws nigh,
        And from th' illumined sky,
      Forth leaning out of air,
      In aspect mild and fair,
      And tones of kindliest care
        He calms their rising fears,
        Proclaiming in their ears,
        While earth, enraptured, hears :

" Glad tidings of great joy I bring !
  News that shall make all people sing !
  For unto you is born a King
    In David's town this night,
    The Lord of glory bright,
    The Saviour, earth's delight,
      Messiah, long-foretold,
      Th' Anointed One of old,
      The Prince of Judah's fold,
      Who brings earth's age of gold."
  Instant all the ether swings
  With the billowy rush of wings !
    Instant all the air around
    Leaps and throbs with rhythmic sound !
    Million smitten strings resound !
  Million tongues the chorus raise,
  Warbling, gushing gusts of praise :
" Glory to God in the highest ! Glory !
  Glory to God ! Earth echo the story !
  Peace upon earth, good-will to man,
  As it was at the first, when time began !
  As it is, when God, as Immanuel born,
  Descends to perish for man forlorn !
  As it now, henceforth and forever shall be !
  Amen, and amen, to eternity !
        To Eternity !
        To Eternity !
  Amen, and amen, to Eternity !"

Thus praising God the anthem rang,
As all the choirs celestial sang ;
   And higher, higher, higher
   Seraphic songs aspire
   In symphonies of fire,
   Till every golden lyre,
   And every conscious wire
   To holiest rapture strung,
   And every flaming tongue
   Unite to swell, the song ;
And all earth's tribes, in farthest climes,
Heard sweetness in all Nature's chimes ;
And all the planets in the sky
Stood listening, as the earth rolled by,
Till rapture thrilled through space afar,
And answers flashed from star to star !
   And still, through Judah's vales
   That anthem swelled the gales,
   Till every mountain-height
   Responded through the night,
   And every cliff of stone
   Sent back the antiphone,
The lingering echoes long
Enthralled th' entangled song
The rocks and glades among,
   And rolled the rapturous strain
   In billows to the plain,
   That rolled it back again,
   Until the sweet refrain,

Lured in romantic dells,
Prolonged through caverned cells,
With one last cadence swells
Above the lonely fells ;
Then languishes along the leas,
And mingles with the midnight breeze,
That whispers peace as on it flees,
And bears the song o'er lands and seas.

V.

THE MEDITATION.

O WONDROUS song, once sung for all the ages,
  How, evermore, thy burden spreads and grows !
How the long line of poets, seers, and sages
  All swell the mighty anthem as it flows !
And crowned kings and holy martyrs singing,
  'Mid flames and torments, tell thy conquering power,
And children's voices, in glad chorals ringing,
  Still hail the rapture of that deathless hour !

Time's central song ! Earth's singers catch thy motion,
  And tune the hymns of centuries to thy sound ;
As rivers draw their fullness from the ocean,
  And pour it back, in one unending round.
The earth-born chants of glory, fame, or pleasure
  Expire as ages roll, nor reach Time's shore ;
But songs that catch Heaven's mighty swing and measure
  Shall sing through earth and Heaven forevermore.

PART SECOND.   THE MAGI.

[Matthew 2 : 1–12.]

I.

THE ARRIVAL.

In summer sunset stood Jerusalem,
Framed round with mountains like a well-set gem,
A mighty cameo carved on Zion's crest,
All bathed in glory from the amber west
That streamed o'er wall and gate, o'er tower and shrine,
Till earthly temples glowed with light divine.

Amid that splendor of departing day,
A stately caravan ascends the way
From Kedron's vale to Herod's royal gate,
A thoughtful train, that moves in solemn state,
On some great errand bent ;—the portal's passed ;—
Silence and twilight wrap the world at last.

II.

THE AUDIENCE.

Lo, in yonder palace hall,
Waiting stand three strangers tall.
Not the Arab, lean and swart,
Not the Hebrew, stout and short,
Not the Egyptian, brown and mild,
Not the Syrian, strong and wild,

Not the Greek, with auburn hair,
Not the Roman's haughty air,
Not the Ethiop's sun-burnt face,
Not the Scythian's savage race,
In the monarch's hall are seen.
Men of calm, majestic mien,
Clad in robes of mystic white,
Greet Judea's King to-night—
Greet him as his equals born,
All too great for slight or scorn.
Seers of Persia's ancient clime,
Here they stand, in port sublime ;
Seers from Zoroaster taught
Through two thousand years of thought,[1]
Poring deep on earth and sky,
And the soul's strange mystery—
Born to mount, a spark of fire,[2]
Deathless still when suns expire !
Sages skilled in all earth's lore
Gathered through the centuries hoar,
Masters of the Magian line[3]

---

[1] The date of Zoroaster is lost in the obscurity of antiquity, but certainly goes back to near the time when the Eastern Aryans left the parent seat on the upper Oxus and became the conquerors of India, in round numbers nearer to 2000 B. C. than 1000 B. C.

[2] The Magian sacred fire was reputedly brought from heaven by Zoroaster. It was a symbol of God, and also of the soul which came from and would return to him.

[3] Astrology was one of the branches of theology at first, and astronomy should never forget its religious origin.

Versed in starry fates divine.
Such the men whose search for God
Now the heights of Salem trod,
Such the seers whose wondrous tale
Bids the astonished tyrant quail.

III.

THE INQUIRY.

"O King of Judah's favored land,
Before thy throne this day we stand
To ask where dwells that child whose birth
Fulfils the eldest lore of earth,[1]
To greet whose reign new stars arise,
And strange conjunctions mark the skies.
For twice a thousand years are gone
Since spake the sage of hoar Irân,
Spitama,[2] far by Oxus' wave,
That one should come the world to save.
For Zerdusht, sent by Ormazd, said
That one whose power would wake the dead
Should rise from out the distant West,[3]
And reign through ages long and blest.

---

[1] Namely, the Eden-lore. See notes on the poem "The World-Wide Hope," pp. 144-153, for much light on this poem.

[2] Spitama was the family name of Zarathrusta, Zerdusht, or Zoroaster, and he is seldom mentioned in the Avesta without the use of this name.

[3] The Iranic prophecies after Zoroaster pointed to the West, and to the descendants of Abraham, for *Zosiosh*, his greatest successor.—*McClintock and Strong, article* "*Magi.*"

And fifteen centuries now have rolled
Since Aram's seer [1] his star foretold,
A sceptred star,[2] with beams benign,
From Jacob's seed o'er earth to shine.
And Judah's captive prince and sage [3]
Who 'scaped unharmed the lions' rage,[4]
Who read th' Assyrian's dreams profound,[5]
And swayed great Cyrus, far-renowned,[6]
Who saved Chaldea's starmen hoar,[7]
And taught our sires profounder lore,[8]
He, helped of favoring heaven, alone
Of mortal men the years made known ;
Gifted from God with glance divine,
He fasted, prayed, and read the sign.[9]
And now, the years fulfilled, behold
The starry sign revealed of old !
For, as we passed from Zagros' height
To Babel's plain, behold by night,
The star of war,[10] the star of peace,[11]
The star of Jove that gives increase,

[1] Balaam's prophecies, Num. 23 : 7 ; 24 : 25 ; especially 24 : 17.
[2] Ibid.   [3] Daniel. See Dan. 1 : 6.   [4] Ibid. 6 : 22.
[5] Ibid. 2 : 31 et seq.; 4 : 19 et seq.   [6] Ibid. 1 : 21 ; 10 : 1.   [7] Ibid. 2 : 24.
[8] Ibid. 2 : 48, "chief governor over all the wise men of Babylon"—*i.e.*, Hebrew *Rab-Mag*, Greek *Archimagos*, President of the Magi, who were of many sects and orders.   As president he was their chief expounder, and in position to teach them the correct Hebrew forms of the Messianic prophecies of Zoroaster.   See McClintock and Strong, article "Magi."
[9] Ibid. 9 and 10.   [10] Mars.
[11] Saturn, in conjunction with Jupiter.   See Upham's "Star of the Wise Men."

Beneath that arch of power and hope
The fiery trigon's horoscope,[1]
Joined thrice their threefold splendor grand
Above Judea's favored land !
And central 'mid their triune blaze
Burst a strange orb,[2] whose dazzling rays
Proclaimed,—so taught Chaldea's sees,—
The finished round of fated years,
That bring th' Anointed, long foretold,
And Earth's far-cycling Age of Gold.[3]
And when the grand portent we saw
Flashed out by heaven's unerring law—
Planets and constellations blent
In that resplendent firmament—
His world-wide sign at last unfurled,
Whose world-old promise cheers the world [4]—
We bowed beneath that splendor's span,
And praised the Lord of heaven and man ;
We sang old hymns of ancient seers,
The hoary songs[5] of nameless years,

---

[1] See Upham's "Star of the Wise Men."   [2] Ibid.

[3] The Gentile "golden age" is in the past, a lost Eden ; that of the Christian is in the future Millennium, an Eden recovered, a "Paradise Regained," as sung by Milton in his noble poem, which would have been considered great, had not "Paradise Lost" been greater. But a Satanic hero will be more fascinating to the world than a divine one for several ages to come.

[4] See works and cyclopædia articles on Gentile prophecy.

[5] Some of the monotheistic hymns of the Vedas and of the Avesta are among the oldest fragments of human thought in existence.

Till, dumb for joy, we gazed and wept—
The mighty, world-old promise kept !
No more the wondering East could hold
Our rapturous thoughts that westward rolled.
The desert saw our midnight march
Still lit by that imperial arch ;
The toiling camels [1] in long line
Instinctive owned the mystic sign,
And turned, without command, each day,
Where Heaven and Nature led the way ;
Till here we stand on Salem's height,
And ask where rests the World's Delight, [2]
What path to him our homage brings,
Born King of Jews, and King of kings."

IV.

THE REVELATION.

A nameless terror on the tyrant fell,
　Who, base usurper, [3] ruled o'er Judah's state !
The false Idumean owned the unknown spell,
　And shook beneath the shadow of his fate !

---

[1] The manifestations of brute instinct, or of brutes led by invisible angels, are among the wonders of psychology. See Balaam's ass and the angel, Num. 22 : 31.

[2] *i.e.* the world-blessing seed of prophecy. See Gen. 12 : 3 ; 22 : 18 ; Matt. 2 : 2.

[3] Matt. 2 : 3. The Herods were all of Idumean or Edomite stock, who obtained and held their power over the Jews by subserviency to the Romans.

Apostate Salem heard the rumor spread—
  A tale to thrill with speechless joy profound !—
She heard, and shuddering shrank, with guilty dread,
  And strange forebodings brooded dark around.

Then spake the monarch : " Call the priests and scribes,[1]
  The skilled expounders of the prophets old,
The august Senate[2] of these anxious tribes,
  To read what seers and oracles have told.

" Tell me, ye mitred pontiffs of your race,
  Who scan the lore of time's primeval morn,
Whence comes th' Anointed, heir of David's place ?
  And say what favored town shall hail him born ?"

Lo ! Judah's white-haired sages swift attend
  The imperious mandate none can disobey ;
O'er many a hallowed presage now they bend,
  O'er many a vision bright, and rapturous lay.

Then came the answer : "Monarch, we unroll
  Seven centuries flight, to Móresheth's[3] rapt seer ;
Read thou, for thou canst read, the sacred scroll,
  That marks Messiah's birth-place bold and clear.

" ' Thou Bethlehem-Ephratah, erst David's town,[4]
  Shall not be least of Judah's princely name ;

---

[1] Matt. 2 : 4.   [2] The Sanhedrin.
[3] Matt. 2 : 5, 6. "Micah the Morasthite," of Móresheth, Micah 1 : 1.
[4] Matt. 5 : 2.

Thy future yet shall dim thy past renown,
  Decreed to changeless, everlasting fame ;

" ' For out of these shall Israel's Shepherd rise,
  Of mortal born, but hailed by seraph lays,
Adored as God through all the earth and skies,
  Whose goings forth are from eternal days.' "

The despot hears ; his dreams of empire wane,
  Vain all his long career of craft and crime ;
Esau [1] and Earth shall bow at Shiloh's fane,
  Whose grandeur looms to fill the world and time.

But that dark mind still gropes amid the blaze
  Of oracles from man and nature given,
A dazzling focus of concentred rays,
  From Jew and Gentile, earth and answering heaven.

V.

THE RECOGNITION.

" Call the seers of Persia now," [2]
  Spake the monarch's tones of wrath ;
Vengeance brooding on his brow,
  Plotting deep a direful scath.

---

[1] Esau, Idumea, the Herods, must fall before Christ.   Herod feels himself already in danger, and the savage Arab in him soon gets the better of the thinly veneered Jew.

[2] Matt. 2 : 7, 8.

"Tell me, wise and holy men,
        When did yon strange star appear?"
Grave and calm, they spake again :
        " Lo, it shineth now a year."

"Speed to Bethlehem ; him ye ask
        Slumbers there in infant grace.
Haste, fulfil your pious task,
        Search with care through all the place.
When ye find him bring me word,
        I would join your pilgrim band ;
Heaven's great heir should be adored,
        Known, revered, through all the land."

Salem's gates once more unfold,
        Winds the throng o'er Judah's hills.
Sunset slants its darts of gold,
        All the soundless silence thrills,
All the pomps of nature wait—
        Wait till twilight zephyrs sigh.
Sudden there, o'er Bethlehem's gate,
        Streams a splendor down the sky.

Lo that star [1] by Oxus hailed,
        Star by Babel's [2] sages read,

---

[1] Matt. 2 : 9, 10.

[2] I bring the Magi from the primitive, prehistoric Irân, on the upper Oxus, to make their year's journey. They stop at Babylon and confer with the Chaldæan astronomers on the way.

All its beams once more unveiled,
  Swims in seas of light o'erhead !
Pours its soft and silvery tide,
  Bathing wall and tower and fane,
Refluent waves that tremble wide
  Over mountain, field, and plain.

Guided by the lamp from heaven,
  On the raptured Magi speed,
Grateful for such witness given,
  They have found the Child indeed.
Now it hangs above the place
  Where his humble roof is spread—
Heir of glory, King of grace,
  Rocked in infant's cradle-bed.

VI.

THE ADORATION.

Lo, the sages prostrate falling,
On the infant Saviour calling.
Wisest seers of far-off nations
Round him blend their supplications.
Praise and prayer like incense pouring,
Rapt, illumed, inspired, adoring !
Hymns of joy with rapture swelling,
O'er and o'er with transport telling
All the weird and wondrous story,
All its faith, its toil, its glory !

Not vain babblers they, with mystic
Signs, and secrets cabalistic ;[1]
Not false wizards, foul, infernal,
Conjuring with the Name supernal ;
Not black magic's league with devils,
Theirs, nor witchcraft's midnight revels ;
Not the stark fakeer's pain-braving,
Not the howling dervish's raving,
Not idolatry's brute vision,
Not the Greek's fond dream elysian.
Men were they whose sires through ages
Kept the world's primeval pages,[2]
Kept and conned the faith once cherished
When a world apostate perished,
And whose kings[3] God's shrine and nation
Reared, with world-wide proclamation.

Men were they whose search had wandered
Wide through nature, prayed and pondered,
Seeking one great truth supernal,
God th' all-perfect, God th' eternal.
Men were they austere and awful,
Men who abhorred th' impure, unlawful ;

---

[1] See works and articles on *Cabala,* or *Kabala,* and Talmud, Magician, etc.
[2] See note 3 on p. 164.
[3] There is no doubt but the purest Aryan monotheism of the earliest Vedic and Avestic hymns was from the same source as the purest Semitic faith of the Hebrews, and that this fact had a powerful effect to make the Persian Empire favor the Jews, and to induce Cyrus and Darius Hystaspes to rebuild Jerusalem.

Men with souls on fire for union
With their Source—sublime communion !
Such were they.   Not souls more fitting
In proud Salem's shrine are sitting—
Souls of nobler, purer merit
Not the globe's wide realms inherit—
Meet to bring earth's best oblations,
Great first-fruits of all the nations.[1]
Homage glad for Him whose greeting
Jew and Gentile join, completing.
Let them bring, and bow, and offer.
Lo, from many a jewelled coffer,   .
Many a casket rare and shining,
Pour forth treasures past divining ![2]

1. GOLD.

And first imperial gold they bring,
Grand service, meet for sceptred king ;
For Him whose right to reign alone,
Wide subject realms with tribute own.
Bright coins of many a mint are there,
And many a blazoned crown they bear ;
Broad arms and seals of towns and states,

---

[1] These Magi were the noblest and fittest ambassadors the whole Gentile world could have furnished to send to greet its Redeemer ; and as representing its future master race, the Aryan stock, they were the blood-kin ancestors and representatives of the Indo-European Christian nations, who rule the learning, power, and wealth of the world for Christ to-day.

[2] Matt. 2 : 11.

From Egypt's Nile to Indus' gates ;
From shores that drink Atlantic's spray
To sands that slope to far Cathay :
Earth's empires round that infant rolled,
Their royal duty paid in gold,
The pledge of Earth's uncounted hoards,
Whose wealth and power are all her Lord's,
Whose mines and gems and treasures won,
Shall serve the kingdom of God's Son.

2. FRANKINCENSE.

Divine frankincense next exhales
Its odor on the ravished gales,
That balsam owned o'er all the earth,
A gift too rare for mortal worth ;
Fragrance too fine for crumbling clod,
And only breathed in flame to God.
That sacred incense heaven denied [1]
To mortal joy or mortal pride,
Beneath the conscious infant's eye
Now rolls its volumes toward the sky,
And sense of Heaven's accepting grace
With joyous sweetness fills the place.
Not spicy gales from Yemen bring
Such balm, while birds of evening sing ;
Not Hermon's cedar, Ural's pine,
Expire so sweet in flames divine ;

[1] Ex. 30 : 34-37.

Nor sandal, fetched from far Malay,
So steals the sense and soul away.
So prayer from contrite souls ascends.
So faith with pure forgiveness blends.
So orisons of souls sincere
Accepted greet Jehovah's ear,
And guilt and pain find glad release,
When heaven's blest Spirit whispers peace.

3. MYRRH.

And now, at last, the myrrh's sad breath
Reluctant sighs of woe and death ;
Of grief and bitterness it tells,
And sorrow in its sweetness dwells.
No flame its pungent soul sublimes,
No temple's arch its vapor climbs ;
No pestle grinds it with sweet spice
To burn—a costly sacrifice.
Its heavy perfumes stifling roll,
Its power benumbs both sense and soul.
The wretch condemned to pangs untold
It soothes with stupors dull and cold ; [1]
E'en rank corruption's hosts obey,
And quit the corpse that owns its sway.
Then why, ah why, this gift of fear,
This omened sorrow, blending here

---

[1] Owing to its powerful anæsthetic and antiseptic properties, it was given to condemned criminals, and used for embalming.

With royal gold and incense sweet,
For King and God a gift complete?
Ah Calvary! thy tale was known
Ere eldest angels hymned the throne!
That lamb, of virgin-mother born,
Was slain ere chaos blushed with morn.[1]
Before the founded world God's plan
Forestalled the sin, the shame of man,
And mercy gave God's only Son
Ere mortal joy or woe begun.
The myrrh before all else is his;
For this he quit the bowers of bliss,
For this the stable heard his cries,
For this he lives, for this he dies.
And royal gold and incense breath
Are his by right of myrrh and death;[2]
For, conquering Death, he yet shall rise
To crowns and anthems in the skies!
O King, O Christ! what sorrows stir,
What raptures, at thy gift of myrrh!

VII.

POSTLUDE.

'Tis done. They give their gifts, they give themselves—
Themselves Philosophy's first-fruits to Faith;

---

[1] Rev. 13: 8. "The Lamb that hath been slain [*i.e.* in the divine plan] from the foundation of the world," Rev. 13: 8, R. V.

[2] Heb. 2: 9, 10; Rev. 5: 9-14.

First-fruits of Science ; howsoe'er she delves,
  Or soars through all that is, above, beneath.
  The universe explored is but the breath
Of that Intelligence [1] incarnate now,
  And minds that scan his power, his love, his death,
His life o'er death, through worlds and æons bow,
And crown with many crowns [2] the great Creator's brow.

'Tis done. Th' adoring Magi, warned by heaven,
  To their own climes return another way.
'Tis done. This mystic sign to mortals given,
  Shall teach the nations to time's farthest day.
  For unknown tribes their homage yet shall pay,
 And mightiest empires on his nod attend ;
  To him shall endless generations pray,[3]
And praise like incense evermore ascend,
Till earth and heaven at last their alleluias blend.

'Tis done. My soul, what offering canst *thou* bring,
  Meet gift for Him who chose the myrrh for thee ?
What fit oblation for such hero-King,
  Who mounts the awful throne of deity ?[4]
  O Child, O Conqueror, hear my spirit's plea !
Teach me thy sovereign, Self-renouncing Love ; [5]
  Help me, by mount or cross, thy path to see,
And, upward drawn, like homeward-circling dove,
A child-like soul, to find Sire, Brother, Home, above.

[1] The Eternal Logos, John 1 : 1–3.   [2] Rev. 19 : 12.
[3] Ps. 72 entire.   [4] Phil. 2 : 9–11.   [5] John 3 : 16.

THE CHRISTMAS BELLS.

I.

Hark ! the bells of Christmas ringing !
All abroad their echoes flinging !
Wider still and wider winging
    On the waste of wint'ry air—
On their solemn, swift vibrations,
Rapture, rapture through the nations !
Rapture, till their glad pulsations
    Million blissful bosoms share !

II.

Every bell to every hammer
Answers with a joyous clamor–
Answers, till from out the glamour
    Of the ages far and dim,
Till from Bethlehem's stable lowly,
Fair as moonrise, opening slowly,
Streams of radiance pure and holy
    Down the brightening centuries swim.

III.

Then the bells ring fine and tender ;
And from out that far-off splendor,
Veiled in light no dreams could lend her,
    Lo, the virgin mother mild,

Pale from guiltless pain unspoken,
Calm in faith's deep trust unbroken,
Bright with heaven's unconscious token,
    Bends above her wondrous child !

IV.

Still the bells ring, softly, sweetly,
Mingling all their chimes so meetly,
Trancing all my soul completely,
    Till the rosy clouds divide ;
And o'er Bethlehem's mountains hoary
Bursts a strange celestial glory,
Swells a sweet, seraphic story,
    Trembling o'er the pastures wide !

V.

Glory ! glory ! God, descending,
Weds with man in bliss unending !
Hark ! th' ecstatic choirs attending
    Smite their lyres with tempest sound !
Shout ! Old Discord's reign is riven !
Peace on earth ! good-will is given !
Shout the joy through highest heaven !
    Make the crystal spheres resound !

VI.

Earth's sad wails of woe and wrangling,—
Like wild bells in night-storms jangling,
Now their jarring tones untangling
    In some deep, harmonious rhyme,—

Touched by Love's own hand supernal,
Hush their dissonance infernal,
Catch the rhythmic march eternal,
    Throbbing through the pulse of time.

VII.

Lo, the babe, where, glad, they found him,
By the chrismal light that crowned him!
See the shaggy shepherds round him,
    Round his manger, kneeling low!
See the star-led Magi speeding,
Priest and scribe the record reading,
Craft and hate each omen heeding,
    Brooding swift the direful blow!

VIII.

Vain the wrath of kings conspiring;
Vain the malice demons firing;
On the nations, long desiring,
    Lo, at last, the Day-star shines!
Earth shall bless the hour that bore him;
Unborn empires fall before him,
Unknown climes and tribes adore him
    In ten thousand tongues and shrines.

IX.

Hark! the Christmas bells, resounding,
Earth's old jargon all confounding!
Round the world their tumult, bounding,
    Spreads Immanuel's matchless fame!

Million hands their offerings bringing,
Million hearts around him clinging,
Million tongues hosanna singing,
    Swell the honors of his name !

X.

Crown him, monarchs, seers, and sages !
Crown him, bards, in deathless pages.!
Crown him King of all the ages !
    Let the mighty anthem rise !
Hark ! the crash of tuneful noises !
Hark ! the children's thrilling voices !
Hark ! the world in song rejoices,
    Till the chorus shakes the skies !

XI.

Living Christ, o'er sin victorious,
Dying lamb, all-meritorious,
Rising God, forever glorious,
    Take our songs and hearts, we pray.
May we, thee by faith descrying,
On thy death for life relying,
Rise to rapture never-dying,
    Rise with thee, in endless day.

PAUL AT PHILIPPI.

[Book of Acts, 16 : 8–15.]

I.

'Twas Sabbath at Philippi's town, in Macedonian Thrace,
But worldly labors, pleasures, strifes, resounded through the
    place ;
For Grecian pageant, Roman power, knew not God's holy day,
And few and strange were Israel's seed, who turned aside to
    pray.

II.

For them no temple reared its dome : Apollo's marble shrine[1]
Rose fair, and from Pangæus' height waved Bacchus' grove
    divine ;
E'en mortal Cæsar's sculptured form[2] obsequious throngs
    adored,
With nature's known and unknown powers, all things, save
    God the Lord.

---

[1] There was an "oracle" of Apollo, as the god of divination, here, as represented by the pythoness, and so undoubtedly a beautiful marble temple. Mt. Pangæus, a spur from Mt. Hæmus, the Thracian Balkan, overlooked Philippi, with a temple and grove of Bacchus or Dionysus on its slope.

[2] The deification of the later Roman emperors, even while living, was ordered by the senate, and practised throughout the empire.

III.

Him, though all-present, those who sought, before his throne
   to wait
In humble prayer and grateful song, must seek without the
   gate ;
And by Gangistes' [1] rippling flood, beneath the summer air,
A lowly group of women [2] bowed to Israel's God, in prayer.

IV.

Not as the wild bacchantes [3] raved among those hills of
   yore,
When first the wine-god's revelries were brought from India's
   shore ;
Not like the Pythoness [4] profane, with Delphic frenzy fired,
Knelt that chaste sisterhood of souls, in worship pure inspired.

---

[1] Gangistes, or Gaggitas, the small river which flowed around the walls of the Philippi of Paul's time. It was a deep and rapid stream there, and flows into a marshy lake in the plain below. See Conybeare and Howson's " Life and Travels of St. Paul ;" also a very copious and thorough article on Philippi in McClintock and Strong.

[2] As a Roman military " colony," under Roman law, there were probably but few Jews there, and they had no synagogue, but only a *proseuchia*, or " praying-place," outside the gate. The larger number of women than men in religious worship has ever been a noticeable fact, creditable to woman.

[3] The worship of Bacchus by the delirious ravings of his priestesses—bacchantes—was here on its classic ground, having been first brought from India to Thrace, and thence to Greece.

[4] The pythoness comes in later in Paul's ministry at Philippi. She is only noticed here for the contrast in favor of these sober and godly women who worshipped Jehovah.

V.

But on that day four [1] holy men sat in their circle small—
Luke, Silas, youthful Timothy, and mighty-minded Paul ;
From Asian climes to Europe's shores that missionary band
Had crossed the Grecian sea to bring glad news, at Christ's
    command. [2]

VI.

From Troy [3] had crossed, by Homer sung in dim primeval yore,
Where Priam built, and Helen sinned, twelve centuries be-
    fore ;
Where Hector, Ajax, Diomed, and wise Ulysses strove,
And great Achilles' spear o'erthrew heroes, and gods above. [4]

VII.

Not as the old Phœnicians [5] came, who sought Pangæus'
    gold,
Nor as once passed, to win the world, the Macedonian bold ; [6]

---

[1] There may have been more, but the four mentioned were almost certainly present.

[2] By the vision seen at Troas, Acts 16 : 9, 10.

[3] The Homeric Troy (Ilium, whence Homer's "Iliad") was then in ruins, and the Alexandria Troas, whence Paul sailed, was a newer city, on a new site, but on the same renowned "plain of windy Troy," with the scenes of the immortal epic all around it.

[4] The exploits of Diomed against Mars and Venus are here, by poetic license, attributed to the spear of Achilles, who was the great hero of the war, the slayer of the Trojan champion Hector.

[5] The Phœnicians wrought the gold mines of Mt. Pangæus before the beginning of the Greek history of the locality.

[6] Alexander the Great.

Not with the pomp of earthly state, nor pride of earthly lore,
Those way-worn pilgrims met that day beside Gangistes'
    shore.

VIII.

That plain, an hundred years agone, saw Rome's Republic [1]
    fall,
When Freedom fled the conquered world, and Tyranny
    grasped all ;
And Hæmus' snow-clad peaks, afar, blushed erst, when
    Typhon [2] strove
And Earth's rude powers, o'erwhelmed in blood by bright
    celestial Jove.

IX.

But ah, that day a mightier than Philip's deathless son,
Or great Augustus, on that plain Rome and the world who
    won,
Or mythic Jove, whose fabled bolts the Titan crew could
    quell,
Was first to Europe preached,[3] as Lord of heaven and earth
    and hell.

---

[1] At the famous battle of Philippi, fought on this plain B.C. 42, when the Republican power fell forever, and Caius Octavius, grand-nephew of Julius Cæsar on his mother's side, became Cæsar Augustus, the first and most famous emperor of Rome.

[2] Mt. Hæmus was the scene of the famous mythological conflict between Jupiter (Jove) and the Titans.

[3] At least this is the first *record* of preaching. There were Christians at Rome, and probably elsewhere in Europe, before we read of any preachers among them, but this is the first official apostolic beginning.

X.

Him Paul proclaimed, of Mary born, the peasant Nazarene,
And told his life of wonders o'er, 'mid that enchanting
    scene ;
Not Orpheus' shell,[1] that thrilled those shores, while trees
    and rocks kept time,
Nor bright Apollo's golden lyre,[2] e'er breathed such strains
    sublime.

XI.

Good news ! glad news ! the Lord is come ! Immanuel, long
    foretold,
Has lived, and died, and risen, and reigns, eternal bliss t' un-
    fold !
And on that list'ning company blest influence benign
E'en now he pours, till many a soul is lit with joy divine.

XII.

And one true heart God opened then, touched by his Spirit's
    power—
A woman's heart, and Lydia's faith found life in Christ that
    same hour ;
And all her wealth, with all her love, she laid at Jesus' feet,
And in her house God's servants found home, church, and
    converse sweet.

---

[1] The triumphs of Orpheus' wonderful harp—whose body was a dried tor-
toise-shell—occurred here in Thrace, where he was a king and poet-minstrel.
[2] Apollo, as the god of the lyre as well as of divination, was also worshipped here.

XIII.

Oh, brightest day that ever yet has dawned o'er Europe's hills,
Thy meek beginning all my heart with hope and comfort fills !
Pangæus' hundred-petalled rose,[1] that sets his slopes aflame,
Breathes not such fragrance as thy deed, around Philippi's
    name !

XIV.

Fade, Grecian glory ! Roman power ! A mightier empire's
    march
Is blazoned on the orient sky, and kindles heaven's high arch !
Rise, Freedom, nevermore to fall ! Rise, woman,[2] pure and
    bright,
To cheer man's toil up centuries of heavenward-deepening
    light !

XV.

And ever when our hearts grow faint, or earthly dreams allure,
When fruit seems small, the cross too great for nature to
    endure,
We'll hail that band who preached and prayed beside Gan-
    gistes' wave,
And trust Him still who reigns for aye, omnipotent to save.

---

[1] The " Rosa Centifolia," " Hundred-leaved rose," mentioned by Theo-
phrastus and Pliny as blooming on the slopes of Pangæus, near Philippi,
blooms there still, as all over southern Turkey, in vast fields, as a staple crop,
in the " attar districts," where thousands of acres are red for weeks with the
roses in their season.

[2] It is interesting to note that the continent where Christianity has done
most for woman is the one where woman first did most for Christianity, at
its introduction.

THE SACRED GLORY OF OLD AGE.

TO THE REV. DANIEL CURRY, DD., LL.D.,

EMANCIPATIONIST, EDITOR, AUTHOR AND LEADER OF THE CHURCH,

whose glorious white head and spotless fame, and his unbroken strength at seventy-six years, make him an illustrious example of its theme, this poem is admiringly and lovingly dedicated.

" Thou shalt come to thy grave in a full age, like as a shock of corn cometh in in his season."
—Job 5 : 26.

" The hoary head is a crown of glory, if it be found in the way of righteousness."—Prov. 16 : 31.

" For as the days of a tree are the days of my people, and mine elect shall long enjoy the work of their hands."—Isa. 65 : 22.

HAIL, blest OLD AGE ! when life well spent is crowned
With years and honors, loved, revered, renowned ;
Earth's noblest state, where all ripe virtues blend,
And life's best hopes in rich fruition end.
So the round year, its hoarded labors won,
Basks 'midst its stores, 'neath autumn's golden sun.
And when white locks and venerable years
Are crowned with holy piety, that cheers
Life's slow decline, and o'er its closing days
Sheds a warm halo of celestial rays,
Then time's supremest gift to man is given,
And, doubly crowned, he tastes both earth and heaven.

How glorious stood earth's patriarchs of old,
While ages lapsed, and centuries unrolled
The long and labored tapestry of time,
Thick wrought with wisdom's golden lore sublime !
Like mighty oaks whose rugged, iron forms,
While ages roll defy the mountain storms,

Towered ADAM, SETH, and ENOS, hand in hand
With CAINAN, JARED, and METHUSELAH grand,
A giant grove, beneath whose shadow stood
An unknown world, from Eden to the flood ;
Whose long tradition kept creation's lore,
And o'er the deluge safe the treasure bore !

See NOAH, prophet, preacher, seer and sage,
Last light of hope that warned earth's blackest age ;
Whose mighty ship outrode a drowning world ;
Great sire of tribes whose standards, far unfurled,
Three continents explore, and nations found
Whose fame shall spread to time's remotest bound ;
Yet age on age they turn to own once more
Earth's second sire, his blessing to implore,
Whose heaven-inspired, benign, paternal sway ·
Gilds realms on realms, that love, revere, obey.

Blest day divine when heavenly strangers trod
The plain where dwelt in peace the " FRIEND OF GOD "
At his tent's door, while passed the sultry hours,
The Patriarch breathed the balm of Hebron's bowers.
Around was peace, and power, and prince-like wealth,
Within were prayer and plenty, honor, health,
Where he and Sarah, save one wish content,
In thankful, pious love life's evening spent.
That wish heaven hears, they clasp their infant boy,
And Isaac fills God's goodness and their joy,—

Isaac, whose offering crowned that faith sublime
Whose grandeur awes the world to endless time !

How glorious in life's golden sunset shows
The MAN OF UZ, the man of mighty woes !
What quivering human heart did God e'er probe
Like that pure, patient heart of godlike JOB ?
A prince of Joktan's tribes, a grand Emír,
Arabia's saint and sage, Jehovah's seer,
He kept the faith from Noah's cov'nant true,
Though Abr'ham's favored race he never knew,—
That faith which Balaam preached, but basely sold—
Apostate ! lost for Balak's bribing gold !
Such he, the mightiest man of all the East,
Whose children's days go 'round in endless feast ;
Whose flocks and herds o'erspread a thousand hills ;
Whose pious soul God's grace with goodness fills—
Hell boldly challenged to impeach his worth !—
Perfect and upright !   Not his like on earth !

Yet, such God's will, this steadfast soul to try,
In one dire charge hell, earth, and blazing sky
Around him crash !   Health, wealth, friends, children, gone,
Bereaved, o'erwhelmed, he sits in dust alone ;
Yet cries : "The Lord who gave hath taken away ;
Blest be the glorious name of God this day !
I know, I know my great Redeemer lives,
And life or death alike in love he gives.

Worms waste this flesh, yet in this flesh I'll see
My God on earth !   He yet shall call for me,
And though he slay me, yet in him I'll trust,
And shout with answering joy from Sheol's dust ;
Or wait till his appointed time shall come,
When he remembers me and brings me home."

The storm rolls by, hell's fierce and envious blast,
And mortal faith towers, triumphs, to the last !
The mystery clears, and God avows with pride
His hero-saint, 'gainst earth and demons tried,
Whose faith a false philosophy [1] reproves,
And owns that God may chasten those he loves.
God's hand afflictions sore full oft may send,
Yet he who sorrows most be most God's friend.
One faithful soul, while God maintains his realm,
All hell may shake,—but not all hell o'erwhelm !
Then doubling blessings on Job's life descend,
And doubling joys his glorious age attend.
His flocks and herds in ampler thousands roam ;
Brave sons, fair daughters, throng his princely home ;
Four generations swell their sire's renown,
And sevenscore years his head with honors crown ;

---

[1] The friends of Job were in that short-sighted error in moral philosophy and theology which, ignoring the retributions of the life to come, suppose that all reward and punishment are in this life, and are therefore bound to suppose that the prosperous here are virtuous, and the unfortunate wicked, a theory which needs only to be stated, in the light of facts, to be refuted. See Christ's rebuke of the same error among the Jews, Luke 13 : 1–5.

Till, full of days, sufficed, the saint sublime
Departs in peace,—revered through earth and time.

How blest was JACOB when he saw, in truth,
Through age-dimmed eyes, his Joseph, lost in youth ;
When Egypt's Lord with pride his sire avowed,
And Egypt's king to crave his blessing bowed ;
When round his dying couch, in reverence grave,
Twelve mighty sons his benediction crave !
Then on his seer-like sight in vision rose
His countless race, triumphant o'er their foes ;—
Their conquering tribes, of Canaan's soil possessed,
A powerful realm through ages long and blest ;—
Till Shiloh's coming fired his passing soul,
And Zion's glory dawned from pole to pole.

Lo, MOSES, graced, not bent, by sixscore years,
Time's matchless son, in fadeless prime appears !
On Nebo's dome, with eyes undimmed and bright,
From Hor's brown crags to Hermon's snow-crowned height
From Syria's sands to ocean's far-off shore,
He views the long-sought country o'er and o'er,—
Jordan's deep vale, that boasts a tropic sun,
Carmel's green ridge, and glorious Lebanon.
What wondrous ways his pilgrim feet have trod
Since, scorning Egypt's crown for Israel's God,
Through fourscore years Jehovah's grace and power
Have led him, safe, to life's last glorious hour !

Before his eyes the hills of promise glow ;
Freed, taught by him, a nation camps below
Proud Egypt slumbers where the sea-waves moan ;
Nations unborn earth's noblest law shall own ;
Jehovah's name adored by man once more—
God's burial here, immortal life before !

CALEB and JOSHUA, faithful erst for God,
In green old age the hills of Canaan trod.
Bold CALEB, valiant at fourscore and five
His pledge fulfils the giant brood to drive
From Hebron's mount.   God nerves his good right arm,
He wins his prize, and safe from all alarm
He dwells revered, a venerated man
Among his honored race,—a powerful clan
Who swayed in after years the judgeship's rod,[1]—
" Because he wholly followed Israel's God."

And mighty JOSHUA led God's conquering host
From Jordan's flood to Canaan's farthest coast.
Before him Jericho's famed ramparts fall ;
The sun stands still on Gibeon at his call ;
And thirty conquered kings his sceptre own,
From Seir's wild crags to cedared Lebanon.
On Gerizim a nation's blessing sounds ;
From Ebal's cliffs a nation's curse rebounds.

[1] Othniel, Caleb's nephew and son-in-law, was the second theocratic judge, the first after Joshua, Judges 3 : 9–11.

God's law is owned the rule of all the land,
And each tribe settled where Jehovah planned.
Then all the tribes attend the hero-sage,
And drink the counsels of his reverend age :
His trembling hands a nation's vows record,
A nation's loyal oath to Israel's Lord.
Life's last work rounds a century's toil and trust,
His own green hill receives the hero's dust.

What honor crowns great SAMUEL's closing day,
Whom Israel's tribes and Israel's king obey :
Predestined seer !   The trembling Eli heard
From infant lips Jehovah's awful word
That doomed his impious sons for crimes abhorred;
And Israel owned the prophet of the Lord.
Philistia flies, and Ebenezer's stone
Proclaims the wondrous victory God's alone.
The challenged tribes his spotless sway attest,
Their history's longest sov'reignty, and best ;
A century's cycle o'er his rule has passed,
God's mightiest judge, the purest, and the last.
He crowns Saul king—no king could fill his room !
A mourning nation bears him to the tomb.

What fame gilds mighty DAVID's parting hours,
Bard, warrior, monarch, mourned by Gentile powers !
A threefold genius crowned his soul with fire,
The sword, the sceptre, and the sacred lyre.

His youthful sling the giant warrior felled,
And countless victories life's long triumph swelled.
He found a weak, obscure, defeated state,
And left a powerful empire, rich and great.
He found a ritual narrow, stern, severe,
And left a hymnal earth and time to cheer.
He sinned, but owned contrition's keenest smart,
Humbled and cleansed, a man of God's own heart.
In glorious age he dies, and leaves behind
A son, the sage, the proverb of mankind.

How great ELIJAH's lightning soul o'ercame
Age, sorrow, death, and leapt to God in flame !
God's grandest seer, whose wrath at Baal hurled
Drought, flame, and whirlwind on a trembling world !
But Baal vanquished, Heaven's pure law restored,
And Israel's God by Israel's tribes adored,
Then home to heaven on angel's wings he flew,—
Who earthly home, love, solace, never knew !

A grateful king o'er old ELISHA bowed
And wept in royal woe, and cried aloud :
" Ah ! Israel's chariot, Israel's horseman thou ! "
Then spake the dying seer : " A mighty bow
And store of arrows quickly hither bring,
And Israel's seer shall shoot for Israel's king ! "
The king obeys.   The mighty bow is bent
By royal hands, the fateful arrow sent :—

" The arrow of the Lord's deliverance flies,
And Syria falls !"—the prophet shouts and dies !—
Buried with royal pomp—whom realms revere,
Kings, nobles, princes proud to bear his bier !
Ev'n in his mummied bones heaven's fires survive,
The dead but touch them and the dead revive ! [1]

See far-famed DANIEL, risen from captive's chains,
An empire's premier through three world-wide reigns !
The mighty monarch's heaven-sent dreams he told,
And time's remotest destiny unrolled.
From Nile to India spreads his powerful sway,
And sixscore provinces his law obey.
The blameless sage, at fourscore years and ten,
Is hurled from power to glut the lions' den :
When lo ! A wonder ! Tamed by angel hand,
With peaceful purr all night the shaggy band
Around the awful saint keep watch and ward,
While Daniel sleeps, or wakes to praise the Lord !
He lives ! He rules ! The Asian world adores ;
And mighty Cyrus' powerful word restores
To Judah's land her tribes and treasures lost,
And builds God's temple at an empire's cost.
Then toil, with life, the " man beloved " lays down,
And fills an unknown grave, a world's renown.

See hoary SIMEON just, devout and pure,
Awaiting Israel's Consolation sure ;

[1] II. Kings 3 : 21.

Nor shall he die—so Heaven's deep whisper told—
Until the Christ of God his eyes behold.
Inspired he seeks with haste the holy shrine,
And there beholds and clasps the child divine !
Then God he praised, the virgin mother blessed—
Though nameless anguish yet should pierce her breast—
And hailed, while seer-like joy his bosom thrilled,
God's great Salvation, on his sight fulfilled,
Heaven's glorious Light, to Jew and Gentile sent :
Then " *Nunc dimittis* " breathed a world's content !

Lo, aged PAUL, in chains at sovereign Rome,
From Nero's bload-stained hand awaits his doom !
Three times Redemption's standard, high unfurled,
His hand has borne around the Grecian world.
On Mar's proud hill,—'neath Dian's world-famed shrine,—
His burning lips have told the tale divine.
The poor, the great, have blessed the tale he brings,
Peasants and peers, philosophers and kings.
The grandest soul of all his living age,
His name sublimest writ on history's page,
Accomplished, learned, heroic, eloquent,—
In chains and dungeons now his years are spent,
Mobbed, stoned, and shipwrecked, exiled, old, and poor,—
Afflictions, bonds, life's only prospect sure,—
And yet o'er all his soul exults on wings,
And like an eagle soars, like seraph sings !
The glorious fight is fought ; the martyrs' faith

Proclaimed and kept !   Now where's thy sting, O Death !
Where is thy victory, Grave !   A crown of life
Awaits the Conqueror in the heavenly strife !

  Last, brightest name that crowns the wondrous band
Where patriarchs, prophets, kings, apostles stand,
Lo, JOHN, beneath a century's spotless snows,
Still breathes that love which through the seraphs glows !
  In youth he owned the mighty Baptist's word,
But, at his mandate, sought th' incarnate Lord.
With James and Peter Hermon's mount he trod,
While Christ transfigured blazed, confessed as God !
His head reclined, beloved, on Jesus' breast,
What time the mournful, mystic feast he blessed.
Last at the cross—first at the empty tomb !—
He stands unawed 'mid shuddering nature's gloom ;
The sacred mother from her son receives—
Executor of all Immanuel leaves
Upon the world he made !—last pledge of love,
Before God's Son shall seek his Sire above.

  Paul's mighty parish,[1] won from Gentile lands,
Obeys the crozier in the patriarch's hands,
Whose fierce rebukes on Gnostic dreams are spent,—
A " son of thunder ! "   Dove and eagle blent !

---

[1] In his later years John became Bishop of Ephesus, with doubtless the whole of Paul's churches in Asia Minor, perhaps those of Greece also, as his diocese, where his philosophic mind found its appropriate field in opposing the rising errors of the greatest early heresy—Gnosticism.

Fierce powers oppose ; the cauldron's bubbling oil
Around his hallowed form forgets to boil,
And o'er his aged limbs refreshing flows,
A sweet anointing, fragrant as the rose !

    Lone Patmos' rocks, and mines, and convict crew,
Touched by the exile, bloom transformed anew,
Changed from that hour, when Christ the sun outshone
In Godhead's awful glory, all his own.
Then on the awe-struck seer what visions broke !
Earth, heaven, and hell around him opening spoke !
Seals ! trumpets ! vials ! dragons ! hosts of light !
The wars of God that shake the world for right !
Earth's farthest ages o'er his vision flash !
He hears great Babylon's world-resounding crash !
He sees the new Jerusalem descend,
God's dazzling church, whose glories ne'er shall end !
And still he lives, the world to teach and cheer,
Earth's last, profoundest, most seraphic seer ;
The Old Man Glorious, seer of love and flame,
Who tarried till his Lord in glory came !

    Such God's old age, for mortal man designed,
The ripening grandeur of flesh, soul, and mind ;
" For as the years that crown some mighty tree,"
His promise runs, " my people's years shall be,"
Where bud and bloom and leaf and fruit appears,
Shook down to bless the world a thousand years !
Such God's grand patriarchs, seers, and sages hoar,

Whose white heads crowned and blessed the world of yore.
O Tully,[1] noblest soul of seven-hilled Rome,
Whose golden periods down the centuries come
Mellifluous, matchless, how thy classic page
Where virtuous Cato praises pure Old Age,
Culling such lives as grace Redemption's line,
Had glowed with noblest ardor quite divine !

But lo ! beyond time's bounds Heaven's rainbowed throne
In glory looms, and like a sardine stone
Or ruddy jasper, He who fills it glows :—
Around his feet, redeemed from sins and woes,
Sit four and twenty ELDERS, mortal forms,
Hoary and white with time's wild years and storms,
Old Men from Earth, who, 'mid that heavenly throng,
Sit next the Lamb, whose faith they kept so long :
Sages and seers and bards and prophets old,
Priests, patriarchs, kings, apostles, martyrs bold,
Heads of the Church, who led her hosts through time,
And now sit next the throne in rest sublime,
And judge the world, whose wrath for Christ they braved,
And rule the blissful nations of the saved,
And join Redemption's song, in endless strains,
To Him whose blood has cleansed all earthly stains !

[1] Marcus Tullius Cicero, the great Roman orator and moralist, whose dialogue, *De Senectute*, " On Old Age," is one of the finest of the Latin classics, both in its sentiments and its style. Cato major (the elder) he uses in the dialogue as his principal speaker.

What were immortal youth to age like this,
Throned, crowned, revered through heaven's long age of
    bliss !

Great Father, hear thy child's adoring prayer :
I ask not age, but if thy wisdom spare
This life, bestowed by thee, to lengthened years,
O make them pure and peaceful, free from fears,
Useful and wise !   When passion's fires are past,
Let nobler flames burn quenchless to the last ;
Valor for right, high scorn of base control,
And eagle ardor kindle still my soul.
Let Christlike goodness, humble charity,
God's gifts alone, take root, bear fruit in me ;
And when at last I sleep beneath the sod,
May this be said : He loved both man and God.
    And when, 'mid millions from earth's every land,
Redeemed and saved, in heaven at last I stand,
Then, lost in reverent rapture, let me gaze,
Adoring "One who is of ancient days ;" [1]
Whose hoary hairs like spotless wool are white,
Blanched with eternities of dazzling light !
Eternal God, yet man revealed in truth,
Heaven's dateless age in sempiternal youth !
Pledge of what heaven's old age for man shall be,
Beholding him, like him eternally ! [2]

[1] Dan. 7 : 9, 10, R. V.   [2] I. John 3 : 2.

ARMAGEDDON.[1]

[Book of Joel 2:2, 10, 30, 31; Revelation 12:7-17; 16:14-16; 19:11-21; 20:1-10; Dan. 12:4; Isa. 11:9.]

I.

THE day of God's great battle
　Is breaking on the world ;
The day when right shall conquer might,
　And wrong to hell be hurled.
The storms that shook earth's midnight
　Lower, though their reign is done,
And ghastly clouds, in blood-red shrouds,
　Are struggling with the sun.

---

[1] Armageddon (Rev. 16: 16). R. V. has Har-Magedon, from Heb. *Har* (Greek *Ar*), *mountain*, and Magedon, the Greek form of the Hebrew Megiddo. Megiddo was on a southern branch of the Kishon, at the southern edge of the plain of Esdraelon, and near the foot-hills of the Carmel range, so that they were near enough to be called the Mountains of Megiddo. It was the scene of the famous victory of Deborah and Barak over Sisera and the Canaanite host of Jabin, and of many other famous battles. (See " Elijah," Part II., VI.) The vision of the seer exalts it into a type of the great universal and final conflict between good and evil in the world. Thus the famous place becomes symbolical, rather than real ; yet, as in all symbols, the groundwork of its mystical signification is in the literal place and its literal history ; hence the value of the original meaning, as explaining and intensifying the world-renowned symbol.

II.

By old Megiddo's mountains,
    On vast Esdraelon's plain,
Where hosts have striven, and realms been riven,
    Since Time began his reign ;
There, in earth's final conflict,
    Before the world shall end,
Shall Good and Ill, and Heaven and Hell,
    A world in arms, contend !

III.

The voice of God Almighty,
    A trumpet-blast sublime,
Peals out on high through all the sky,
    And startles every clime ;
And lo ! through all the nations,
    Where'er the watchword flies,
O'er hill, and plain, and ocean main,
    The mustering millions rise !

IV.

I see the mighty gath'ring
    Of uncomputed bands ;
Prophet and sage, from every age,
    The living of all lands ;
And glorious hosts of martyrs,
    For God and Freedom slain,
From dust revive, start up alive,
    And mingle on the plain !

V.

The great and good, the heroes
  Who toil and die for man,
From every land illustrious stand,
  And tower along the van ;
Not all in earth's high places,
  Not all the sons of fame,
But all well known before God's throne,
  And called by Christ's own name.

VI.

No arms have all these millions,
  No sword, nor spear, nor shield ;
But mightier far the weapons are
  With which they win the field ;
For Truth, and Love, and Labor
  Are more than shield or sword ;
And they shall stand at God's right hand
  Who conquer by his word.

VII.

But see ! another army
  Is mustering for the fight,
And earth and hell its numbers swell
  In dark and wrathful might ;
The hosts of Gog and Magog,
  And armies of the air,
Demons, and ghouls, and damnéd souls,
  That rave in fierce despair.

VIII.

Kings of the earth, old despots
   Who long have bruised mankind,
And long withstood with chains and blood
   The chainless march of mind ;
And dire, gigantic systems
   Of error blind and hoar,
On Christian land new-marshalled stand,
   And threat the world once more.

IX.

And O, woe ! woe ! to mortals !
   For Satan, in great wrath,
From war in heaven by Michael driven,
   Has fall'n in lightning scath ;
And all his dragon-angels,
   A vengeful cloud and vast,
In fury fly through all the sky,
   And swell the blackening blast.

X.

But hark ! A voice from heaven
   Proclaims in triumph loud,
" Salvation, strength, are come at length,
   The kingdom of our God !
The Old Accuser, vanquished,
   From heav'n by martyrs hurled
Who owned the Lamb through death and shame,
   Descends to vex the world !"

XI.

But short shall be his triumph,
  For lo ! heaven's gates unfold,
And hosts of light, on steeds of white,
  March down the streets of gold ; .
And at their head, o'ercircled
  By million arching wings
Flaming all sides, majestic rides
  The Lamb who victory brings.

XII.

And on his radiant vesture,
  And on his mighty thigh,
Stand writ in flames his glorious names,
  That blaze through earth and sky :
" FAITHFUL AND TRUE !" for righteous
  His sceptre, or his rod ;
" THE KING OF KINGS AND LORD OF LORDS !"
  Th' eternal " WORD OF GOD !"

XIII.

And lo ! the great archangels,
  With cohorts bright and fair
Of cherubim and seraphim,
  Come marching down the air !
And far o'er plain and mountain,
  O'er many a field and flood,
Wide o'er the world now floats unfurled
  The banner stained with blood.

XIV.

Up! up! ye saints of Jesus,
  And make your vestments white ;
And girt with flame, in God's great name,
  Urge on earth's final fight !
That ensign o'er you flying
  Must never, never fall,
Till Christ shall reign o'er earth and main,
  Saviour and Lord of all.

XV.

Your burning testimony,
  Born of the Holy Ghost,
And Christ's own blood, a cleansing flood,
  Shall arm your conquering host ;
Until the ancient Dragon,
  By God's strong angel bound,
In judgment's chain, is hurled amain
  Down to the gulf profound.

XVI.

Shut up and sealed in darkness
  The venomed serpent hoar
Who swayed so long the world by wrong
  Shall vex the earth no more ;
Then shine the thrones in heaven,
  Then rule the saints below,
Till truth and peace and righteousness
  Make earth transfigured glow.

XVII.

Then to and fro with gladness
  Shall willing thousands run,
To tell o'er earth Immanuel's birth,
  His great Redemption won ;
The knowledge of Salvation
  Shall spread like seas abroad,
Till onward roll from pole to pole
  The triumphs of our God.

XVIII.

O blissful age !   It hastens !
  It looms in light afar,
And darts a ray of heavenly day
  O'er wrong, and woe, and war.
O joy ! O martyred brothers,
  Your great reward appears !
Up ! live ! and reign with Christ again
  A thousand golden years !

A VISION OF THE AGES.

I.

Down the ages, dim and olden,
Where the shadows, gray and golden,
Gather, till they melt and mingle
Like the shades in dell and dingle
When the twilight, gently closing,
Kisses earth to soft reposing,
Down those ages, dim and olden,
Through those shadows, gray and golden,
Oft in thought I roam and ponder,
Dream, and long, and love, and wonder.

II.

One bright day in brown October,
While the sunlight, sad and sober,
Sweetly sad, and sinking slowly,
Streamed through all my chamber lowly,
Thus I sat—old tomes around me—
Sat as if some spell had bound me—
Turning slow the solemn pages
Of old books, whose lines are ages ;
Books where Time has loved to linger,
Writing dim, with dusky finger,

Wisdom weird, and high, and hidden,
Wealth to half the world forbidden.
Thus, while slow the sun was sinking,
Still I sat, in fancy linking
Thought with thought, till, as in dreaming,
All my thinking changed to seeming ;
And from all the glint and gloaming,
Where my thickening thoughts were roaming,
Gathering grand around and o'er me,
Lo, a glory grew before me ;
And from out the glimmering glory
Souls, sublime in song and story,
One by one, serene and solemn,
Passed, in long, illustrious column !

III.

First the bards, the master-makers,[1]
Souls who saw with open vision
Nature, Hades, worlds elysian,

---

[1] The word poet is a Greek word, *poiētēs*, a maker, from the verb *poieō*, to *make*, to *produce*, to *create ;* whence the idea of original imaginative creation is at the bottom of any true conception of poetry, and without the creative invention of a great imagination there can be no great poem.   But this attribute shows itself in the small as well as the great things of poetry.   It takes creative power to make a blade of grass, as really as to make a planet, and Milton's college poem on the miracle at Cana :

" The modest water saw its God and blushed,"

betrays the imagination that created " Paradise Lost," the most colossal poetic creation of the world, not in bulk, but in conception and character.

Truth, and Beauty ; born partakers
Of a baptism, a libation
From the Fountain of Creation.

IV.

First came two, alone, imperial
Monarchs of the race ethereal ;
Great high-priests of song, whose numbers,
Like the sea, that never slumbers,
Pour their fiery undulations
Through all ages and all nations !
One was crowned, and one was crownless,
One enthroned, the other throneless ;
One by God's own hand anointed,[1]
Ruled a race by Heaven appointed ;

One, in song his peer and brother,[2]
Blind to earth and blind to heaven,[3]
Nature's impulse only given,

From one island to another,
Roamed, and sang his deathless pæan
'Round th' immortalized Ægean.

V.

Then came prophets, patriarchs, sages,
Seers from all the lands and ages :

[1] David.
[2] Homer, to whom ordinary chronology assigns a date from one to two hundred years after David.
[3] That is destitute of Hebrew revelation.

He who walked with God, translated ;
He who saw a world, heaven-fated,
Sink beneath the sea, whose billow
Rocked him, safe as cradle-pillow ;
He the " Friend of God," whose spirit
All the sons of faith inherit ;
Thou, O sage and seer, who standest
Foremost of mankind, and grandest ;
Who, in life's triumphant morning,
Earth's proud thrones and homage scorning,
Siding with a downtrod nation,
Wrought their great emancipation !
Smote th' oppressor's land with wonder,
Hail, and fire, and death, and thunder !
Passed the ocean ; cleft a fountain
From the rock ; and, from the mountain,
Gave the law of God, whose pages
Scatter light through all the ages !

VI.

Seers from other lands and races
Passed me next, with longing faces :
Great Lycurgus,[1] Minos,[2] Manu ;[3]

---

[1] Lycurgus, legislator at Sparta, eighth century B.C.
[2] Minos, mythological king and legislator of Crete.
[3] Manu, the real or mythological author of " The Institutes of Manu," the great Hindu Code in twelve books, dating about 900 or 1000 B.C.

Sage Gautama ; [1] old Kong-fu-tse ; [2]
Older still, the wondrous Fuh-he ; [3]
   And the seers of Brahm and Vishnu ;
Seers Egyptian, seers Chaldean,
Parsees, Magi, priests Sabean,
Rapt, transcendent Zoroaster,[4]
Divine Plato, and his master.[5]

VII.

Who shall say that to no mortal
Heaven e'er op'd its mystic portal,
Gave no dream, or revelation,
Save to one peculiar nation ?

[1] Gautama, the founder of Buddhism, died in India 543 B.C. See note on him on page 146.

[2] Kong-fu-tse, the Chinese form of the name Latinized as Confucius, the great ethical philosopher of China. Died 478 B.C.

[3] Fuh-he (who must not be confounded with Fo, the Chinese Buddha), the reputed founder of Chinese civilization, author of the cosmological "Book of Changes." His alleged reign dates about 2952 B.C., a little longer before Confucius than Confucius is before ourselves. His date is not far from the Septuagint date for Noah, whom he resembles in many particulars. His treatise is monotheistic, teaching an invisible and infinite author of all things. It will surely attract more critical study in coming time.

[4] Zoroaster, or Zarathustra (Persian *Zerdusht*), was the founder of the ancient Persian religion, represented by the modern Parsees (Persians) of India and elsewhere. His date is lost in the prehistoric obscurity of eastern Iran, but no part of the *Avesta* ("Holy text"), the older parts of which he doubtless wrote, and which is about double the size of Homer's Iliad and Odyssey combined, is more recent than 400 or 500 B.C. Hardwick ("Christ and other Masters") dates it back to 700 B.C.

[5] Socrates, "The most Christian of the Philosophers," who revolutionized philosophy.

Souls sincere, now voiceless, nameless,
Knelt at altars fired, and flameless,
Asked of Nature, asked of Reason,
Sought through every sign and season,
Seeking God ; through darkness groping,
Waiting, striving, longing, hoping,
Weeping, praying, panting, pining,
For the light on Israel shining !
Oh, it must be !   God's sweet kindness
Pities erring human blindness,
And the soul whose pure endeavor [1]
Strives toward God shall live forever ;
Live by the great Father's favor,
Saved through an unheard-of Saviour.

VIII.

Then the throng grew vague and vaster,
Moving, mingling, floating faster :
Warriors, heroes, conquerors marching
Laurelled 'neath triumphal arching ;
Statesmen, orators whose thunder
Rent the tyrant's chains asunder ;
Painters whose supreme creations
Ravished the admiring nations ;
Sculptors whose divine ideal
Glorified the living real !

[1] Acts 10 : 35.

IX.

Still, as still I saw or slumbered,
Onward swept the throng unnumbered ;
Forms the world's great heart has cherished,
Forms it never knew, that perished,
Left unknown, to pine and languish,
Drowned in agony and anguish.
Oh, there have been souls celestial
Tortured here in chains terrestrial,
Bound in iron, crushed and broken,
Souls that, could they once have spoken,
Once breathed out the flame that burned them,
Nations had in gold inurned them ;
Countless lips their names caressing,
Endless hearts their memory blessing !
These I saw, their names I knew not,
From their lives the vail I drew not,
But I saw them robed in whiteness,
Walking in serenest brightness,
And I knew that all their sadness
Now was changed to glorious gladness.

X.

Then before my vision, slowly,
Came a humble band [1] and holy.
Few they were, unknown in story,
Crowned with no ancestral glory,

---

[1] I. Cor. I : 26–29.

Poor, unlearned, derided, taunted,
Hated, beaten, hissed, and haunted,
On a convict's cross relying,
Scorned while living, cursed when dying.

XI.

Yet o'er all earth's rage and railing,
Still I saw that cross prevailing !
Seas of blood around it pouring,
Seas of flame around it roaring,
Wet with tears, yet unforsaken,
Still it towered sublime, unshaken,
Rose o'er night, and storm, and terror,
Chased the goblin glooms of error,
Rose in radiance, grew in'glory,
Conquered science, song, and story,
Conquered kingdoms, ransomed races,
Brightened all earth's darkened places,
Bade the sorrowing sigh no longer,
Made man freer, nobler, stronger,
Broke the chains of hoar oppression,
Healed the wounds of old transgression,
Preached the PRINCE OF PEACE, whose praises
Half the world, redeemed, now raises ;
And whose sovereign sway transcendent,
Soon o'er all shall reign resplendent,
Till all nations fall before Him,
And all tribes of earth adore Him.

XII.

Then cried I, O kingdom glorious !
Haste, and reign o'er all victorious !
Fade fond dreams of fame and fortune,
This new empire be my portion !
Fade the pomp of earth's old ages,
Sensual songs, and sensual sages ;
Sensual all, impure, unholy,
Dying from earth's memory slowly.
Let them die ; once I adored them,
Now no more my heart can hoard them.
Once well-nigh had these undone me,
Now a holier hope has won me.
Pass, vain vision of earth's beauty,
Hail, high, holy, heavenly DUTY !
Hail that CROSS ! tear-stained and gory ;
Hail its death, its shame, its glory !
All my heart falls down before it,
All my mind and soul adore it ;
All I am to this be given,
This be mine, on earth, in heaven !

THE PROPHECY OF WISDOM :[1] A PHILOSOPH-
ICAL ODE.

THE ARGUMENT, AND THE CHALLENGE OF WISDOM.

WHEN from the dust, while spheres celestial sang,
Beneath God's hand man's form terrestrial sprang,
With the same breath that breathed the vital flame
Of brute existence through his mortal frame,
From Being's Fount a twofold life[2] was given,
And mind, immortal, crowned him heir of heaven.
    The Sons of God, in glad surprise,
    Shouted for joy through all the skies ;[3]
      The harps of God awoke
      To raptest seraph's stroke,

[1] In this title and poem the term Wisdom is used in the sublime and mystical sense of the Solomonic books, and of that noble apocryphal book, the Wisdom of Solomon, worthy to be canonical for the sublimity of most of its matter. As to whether the term is synonymous with the Greek *logos*, and means the eternal Logos, the Divine Word, I leave to more critical authorities ; but I so understand it. The term Prophecy is also here used in the same archaic sense, implying not necessarily prediction, but divine discourse. The poem is thus, in reality, a discussion of the world-old question of Philosophy and of the Soul : "What is the Chief Good for Man ?"

[2] See Gen. 2 : 7, where the word life is in the dual-plural in the Hebrew —" breath of *lives* "—viz., animal and spiritual.

[3] Job 38 : 7.

Till from their strings of gold
Harmonious rapture rolled
    Up to the white
    Unuttered height
    Of steadfast light,
  Unpierced by creature sight,
Where the Infinite, to the Infinite alone
Revealable, confessed in part, yet all unknown,
  Forever fills the Universal throne.
They sang the immortal mind of man, whose birth
  Forged a new link in being's golden chain,
Crowned with new grandeur this unpeopled earth,
  And taught the choir of worlds another strain ;—
The mind of man, sole master of this globe,
  A splendid planet built to match his will,—
Mind wrapped in matter as a swathing robe,
  But quenchless, deathless, all ethereal still ;
    Launched forth alone, chained to this star,—
    His cradle, and his triumph car,—
      Remote from worlds around,
      No fellow-spirits found,[1]
        Save his own kind ;
        With bestial mind
Below him grading down through every form
Of life and instinct, to the mole and worm ;
Distinct from all by boundless gulfs he stands,

---

[1] Gen. 2 : 20.

With angel mind, and earthly hands ;
A toiler for two worlds, of both compiled,
'Twixt brute and seraph, stands Jehovah's latest child.
　　Who shall instruct him ?   Who
　　　　His soul inform,
　　　　His spirit warm,
　　And teach him to subdue
The brute within him, till the seraph rise
　　Beyond this darkling earth and skies,
　　And seek companionship above,
　　In unknown worlds of light and love ;
Or find, in fitness for that nobler sphere,
A life celestial bursting on him here ?
Who shall unlock his being's mystery ?—
　　　What, whence, this *I* in me ?—
　　　Whence comes the world we see ?—
　　　What is the life to be ?—
　　　What is eternity ?—
Has space diviner worlds, from sorrow free ?—
　　Are other worlds more fair,
With brighter forms of being basking there ?—
　　What, in this world, is best,
　　Which most can make man blest ?—
What is the bliss that orbs his being's scope,
That fills his loftiest firmament of hope,
Refines, sublimes, exalts his nature's whole,
Great as his worth, enduring as his soul ?—
Ye Fates and Powers that rule o'er nature's plan,

Stand forth, make answer to the soul of man !
Ye listening worlds the awful quest attend,
'Tis WISDOM calls, man's highest guide and friend.

ANTISTROPHE I.

THE ANSWER OF PLEASURE.

PLEASURE stood forth, a rosy, flower-crowned sprite,
    With eyes forever brimming o'er with laughter ;
Her wings were like the rainbow's braided light,
    Her voice was song, with harp-strings quavering after.
        "Being is BLISS !" she cried ; .
        " Come, revel at my side !
            Sorrow is death !
        Come quaff my charméd breath !
        Beneath my power
The Universe shall open like a flower ;
Thou, like the bee o'er dew-drops that reflect her,
Shalt roam from world to world and feed on nectar.
    The raptures and delights of time
    Dance to my lute in dulcet rhyme :
            I sip on wings
            Sweets without stings,
            And loves that never cloy
            Are mine without alloy :
Clasp me, and launch on shoreless seas of joy.
Clasp me, and drown in all-entrancing beauty,
All dreams of toil, each dull demand of Duty !

Thou, while Care's dog-star 'neath thee smites and rages,
Shalt drift on amber streams down summer ages.
Sense, sound and sight and scent and taste and touch
    Shall thrill, ecstatic, at each fleshly portal ;
And when love faints, with sweetness overmuch,
    Fancy shall mount on wings of fire immortal ;
And unknown sensuous worlds, like stormless harbors,
Shall woo thee, sateless, through elysian arbors.
PLEASURE is life, fit for the gods supernal ;
Clasp me, and thrill with ecstasies eternal !"

ANTISTROPHE II.

THE ANSWER OF KNOWLEDGE.

Next KNOWLEDGE spake.   Her brow was like the drifts
    Of calm white cloud, that sail the skies of June ;
Her eyes like planets, gleaming through their rifts,
    Unblenched and eager 'mid the blaze of noon.
    "Come, if thou wilt," she said, "and share the boon
I give to all who take it.   Read this earth
    On which thou ridest without sound or shock,—
Itself almost a sun, to you admiring moon ;—
        Read all its leaves of rock :
Read all its changes backward to their birth,
        Its elemental strife
        Of atoms, order, life,
From chaos and from nothing ; all the forms
Of complex life its generous bosom warms ;

Trace through time's labyrinth thy own high race,
Read all its tongues and records. Read the space
That spreads around thee, populous with suns,
       Where each in glory runs,
Leading a glittering host of worlds like thine,
       By the same hand divine,
Sown radiant as foam bubbles o'er the deep.
   Read all the mystic laws that keep
Those flocks of worlds, led forth as shepherds guide their
    sheep.
         Read thy own soul ;—
       What awful problems roll
Their shadows round thy destiny.   Thyself,
What art thou, strange, audacious, earth-born elf?
       What is it sits within
       This living manikin,
And calculates the comet's calendars,
  And with the spectroscope's alembic shows
  Each element that in Arcturus glows,
And counts and weighs and crucibles the stars ;
And on the two legs of a triangle
       O'erleaps the orbit bars
Of whirling suns, and walks self-taught and well,
       Stretching its gunter's chains
       Across star-dusted plains,
And then lies down and sleeps in this skull-cell?
       Who art thou ? and what lies
       Behind thy fleshly eyes?

A quivering drop, a formless protoplasm ?
Can this bridge mind and nature's soundless chasm ?
      An automatic dance
       Of atoms ruled by chance ?
  A glow of ethers in a lobe of brain ?
A grinning monkey's tailless progeny—
Came thus the soul's Promethean spark to me ?—
Let those who to such ancestry aspire
Exult themselves !—I boast a nobler Sire !—
A storm of fire-mists whirled through infinite deeps
   Eddying to worlds, dissolved in mists again ?
       Is this the guess that leaps
          Cause, mind, and God,
       And spurns the topless steeps
Of thought where eldest seraph never trod ?
    Is this the ALL ?   What reigns above ?
Is being's law *chance, destiny,* or LOVE ?
    What love ?—   Whose love ?—   Say, is there ONE,
    In whom all is, by whom all done ?
    Without whom naught, or was, or is,
    Or shall be, through the eternities ?—
    Who *is,* and therefore all things are ?—
    Who wills, and worlds roll, without jar,
       Where nothing was,
       Save He, the CAUSE,—
     In whose calm, infinite might
Suns rise and gleam as motes in summer light ?
Art thou from Him ? To Him returns thy breath ?

Know'st thou this problem, vast and dim ?
Is there a GOD ?   Art thou from him ?
Him canst thou know ? and know that he knows thee ?
Him canst thou show ?   Unmask Infinity ?
Know, know then him, and utter what he saith !
KNOWLEDGE is life !   Dark Ignorance is death ! "

ANTISTROPHE III.

THE ANSWER OF ART.

ART touched the wondrous lyre,
    Her eyes of dreamy fire
Half-closed, seemed fixed on things serene and high,
    Unknown in earth or sky.
Her senses all are double.   Outward forms
To her are veils of one wide life, that warms
Plastic through all things, nature, life, and mind,
Distinct in each, yet one in all combined.
That life is *Beauty*, and its mystic shrine
Is in the Beauty Infinite, Divine.
    Art touched the wondrous lyre :—
"Come learn of me," she whispered in soft tone ;—
The breathing statue burst its shell of stone !
The painted goddess sighed her conscious fire !
    And as the song swept higher,
    Arches and temples rose sublime,
    And pyramids defying time ;
    Minster, cathedral, Parthenon,
    Blossomed while centuries swept on,

Pure marble flowers of human thought,
Hints of the soul, in granite wrought.
And when the forms of matter failed expression,
When color, form, and vastness could no more,—
When music's glorious swell died on thought's shore,
And eloquence itself grew dumb
At truth and beauty's nameless sum,
Then song alone, art's first and last progression,
Caught up creation's anthem sung of yore !
Imagination walked new worlds among,
And Nature found a tongue,
And the soul sung,
And throbbing seraphim their censers swung,
While Art in raptured wedlock bound
Beauty and thought and rhythmic sound,
And bade the pulses of a soul
Through Nature's thrilling framework roll,—
The nameless throb of life divine
When genius fires the mystic line !—
And stole the essences of all bright things
For garlands, crowns, and wedding rings,
And cried, with sunrise in her lambent eyes,
" Beauty is life !   Beauty is bliss !
I rule the universe by this !
The beautiful itself is good,
Beauty is power !   Beauty is god !
Beauty is god !   ART reigns, and chaos dies !"

ANTISTROPHE IV.

THE ANSWER OF PHILOSOPHY.

PHILOSOPHY divine
Rose slow, with port benign,
And soul serene, deep, passionless and still.
She stood a space remote, upon a hill,
In stature of sublimest mould,
And steadfast eyes of clearest truth,
And brow of cloudless, endless youth,
For centuries cannot make her old.
Her voice was like a chime of wondrous bells,
When some grand anthem swells,
Far, solemn, sweet, through groves and vales and dells.
"Come sit by me," she said ;
" Beneath my gaze, as on a map outspread,
Lie all the secret principles of things,
The forces, that like hidden springs,
Impel and guide this universal frame
Which men call Nature :   Undiscovered name !
Beneath my gaze the causes lie
Of all events, in earth or sky ;
The reason of all change, its how, and why,—
And why-not,—for I claim
Negation needs its reason all the same.
They who deny
At Reason's court, must give a reason why,
As they who do affirm ;
For only thus is found CAUSATION'S FINAL TERM.

That search is mine ;—
And not alone *what* is, but *why*,
And *whence*, and *whither*, are my quest :
Thought's most profound behest
Waits my reply.
Through mind and nature up to the Divine
My clew shall guide
The reverent soul who walks obedient at my side.
Reason still bears my torch :
Her mild beams never scorch
The clear-eyed pilgrim seeking truth's high goal.
Beyond the outward husks of things
I lead to being's inmost springs.
Past all phenomena like waves that roll,
I seek creation's steadfast, undiscovered pole.
I climb the final Alps of being,
Olympian peaks, past mortal seeing ;
And he who mounts with me till mists are past,
Shall find th' eternal *Absolute*,[1] at last,
The one unchanging Fount of matter, force, and soul.
Mount, mount with me !"   Philosophy still cries,
" Reason is godlike life !   Unreason dies !"

Antistrophe V.

THE ANSWER OF POWER.

A blast of trumpets dinned my ears !
I caught the echoing roar of cheers !

[1] See Sir William Hamilton's " Philosophy of the Absolute," in his " Lectures on Metaphysics."

A roll of drums !
A shout—" He comes !"
" Power !   Power !   Make way !" stentorian heralds cried.
Back surged the obsequious tide
Of cheering thousands, and a space full wide
Opened ; and lo ! illustrious from afar,
Blazing like dawn, an all-refulgent car,
A throne sublime, untold by art or story,
Rolled onward down a pave of beaten glory,
Flashing iridean splendors, rainbow-vaulted,
Above the burning stars of God exalted ! [1]
Power ! Power !   All grandeurs in his person strove ;
   The might of Hercules was in his frame ;
Apollo's grace, the majesty of Jove,
   His locks ambrosial, and his eyes of flame ;
His voice—melodious thunder ; his right arm—
Olympian to smite, Adonian to charm.
               "Mount to my side !
         All things are mine !" he cried.
         Ride on my throne,
   And call the prostrate world thy own !
Wealth ?—   'Tis the bribe I toss to my poor slaves !
   Gold ?—   'Tis the pavement for my jasper wheels !
Honors !—   I shower them cheap on fools and knaves !
   Rank, titles, place ?—are his who humblest kneels !
         What are all these to me ?
         I sit like Deity !
My glance bids kingdoms rise, and empires fall ;

[1] Isa. 14 : 13.

I rule this rolling ball ;
I. throne its dynasties,
And dash its emperies,
And bid its millions tremble at my call.
The sweets of all its climes are mine,
I quaff its centuries like wine ;
Its beauty, genius, labor, lore,
Are but the toys that trick my store ;
Its arts, that glow when history dies,
Proclaim my touch that bade them rise ;
Its deathless, time-entrancing lays
Are but the epics of my praise ;
And all the mighty toils
Of all the ages are my garnered spoils.
An hundred nations grew to swell Rome's state,
And Rome expired to make one Cæsar great !
Grasp me ! Grasp me !
I'll thrill thee with a sense of deity !
All pangs, all ecstasies, all bliss
Of time, are swallowed up in this.
Weakness expires if I but nod,
Power, Power is this world's god !"
" Power, Power is god !"—realms, races, ages cried ;
And Power stood deified !

EPODE.

THE ANSWER OF WISDOM.

No more hoarse trumpets stunned the shattered air,
　The Babel shout of myriads seemed a jest ;
The earth grew silent as a whispered prayer,
　While day's last embers burned along the West.—
　Yet one deep longing, sateless, unrepressed,
Cried like a lost child, through heart, soul and mind ;
And is this all ?—I moaned, in anguish blind ;—
　Ah then, not yet immortal man is blessed !
　Not these suffice, were all at his behest !
Not worlds on worlds can fill the gulf within his breast !
　　　Amazed, o'erwhelmed, distressed,
　　　I sank, with grief oppressed,
　　　And sighed for endless rest.
'Neath autumn woods, on earth's kind bosom prone,
I lay, while o'er me rushed a woe unknown,
Lay sobbing, crushed, till all the sunset's flame had flown,
　　　And twilight reigned alone.
Then from the soundless infinite there stole
A voiceless whisper sweet through all my soul.
From nameless depths, beyond the speechless stars,
A far, inaudible anthem's dying bars,
Soft as the wind-harp's last expiring stress,
Breathing unknown, supernal tenderness :
And pitying love, that Nature never knew,
Sank like an ether all my being through.

No form, no vision, rose revealed,
All earthly sense was closed and sealed ;
But like the balm when buds of rose,
With silent dawn, their hearts unclose,
A sacred, infinite repose
Filled all my being, its profoundest deeps
Lay like calm coves, where Ocean's flood-tide sleeps,
While not a ripple o'er its glassy smoothness creeps.
        Then WISDOM, from the silence, said,
    " Child, I was with Jehovah when he laid
            Creation's corner-stone ; [1]
Before all creatures I was his alone,
            His loved, his own.
        As one brought up with him of old,
    I saw the unborn universe unrolled
            In archetypal thought,
    Ere molten suns in God's white forge were wrought ;
    Before the first archangel sprang from nought.
    When from God's breath forth flamed the seraphim,
    I tuned their untried harps and infant hymn.
    When fiery chaos streamed before his WORD, [2]
            The uproar wild I heard.
    When, at his fiat, matter, force, and law
            Bloomed into worlds, I saw.
    That fiat smote the abyss, and drift on drift
    Of clustering suns [3] flashed forth as sparkles swift,

----

[1] Prov. 8 : 22-36.   [2] Gen. 1 : 1, 2 ; John 1 : 1-3.   [3] Gen. 1 : 3, 14.

Cleaving the ancient dark with golden rift.
When his wide compass [1] swept the arch of heaven,
And traced their orbits for the circling seven,
I marked their flight.   I watched him while his hand
Scooped out earth's seas and heaved her solid land,[2]
Settled her mountains, gave her deeps their bound,
And taught her changeful year its fruitful round.
   I saw the oak and palm
Rise like green hymns in the third morning's [3] calm.
   I saw the living tribes of earth
   Leap from the hand that gave them birth,
     And walk, or swim, or fly,
     Till earth and sea and sky
   Swarmed populous with sinless mirth.
I saw the Triune counsel crown the eternal plan,
And heard the words sublime go forth, " *Let us make man.*"
 I saw man stand majestic, like his God,
  Last, fairest, noblest triumph of creation ;
 The golden mean of being, from the sod
  Towering to archangelic exaltation.
 I saw his future, from his Eden station,
Stretch through time's ages like a cloudy sea :
 I saw his sin, his ruin, his salvation,
His fate, self-chosen for eternity.
   I saw his agony and shame,
   I saw his triumphs and his fame,

---

[1] Prov. 8 : 27. [2] Ibid. 24, 29. [3] Gen. I : 11, 20-24, 26, 27.

His tears, his bitterness and sorrow,
    The devious paths of life he chose,
His dark to-day, his bright to-morrow,
    His transient hour of joys and woes,
The infinite glory waiting for his winning,
All these I saw before creation's first beginning.
        I saw man's FINAL GOOD,
Not pleasure, knowledge, art, philosophy, or power,
        But *to be like his God*,
        As once erect he stood,
In all the grandeur of his primal dower,
Pure and self-poised in truth and virtue, free ;
Epitome sublime of Deity.
        All this my deep eyes scan ;—
Thus WISDOM answers to the soul of man :—
        False *Pleasure* flatters to deceive ;
        Knowledge no heart-cry can relieve ;
        Art gilds man's misery, not removes ;
        Philosophy his fall but proves ;
        And all the boast of earthly *Power*
        Is but the phantom of an hour,
Fading, dissolving, changing, mocking all,
Like lovers' ghosts, when dreaming lovers call.
Is then man wronged ? his being worse than vain ?—
The universe a cheat ?—extinction gain ?—
Creation frustrate, folly, or a crime,
With man so far from heaven, so weak to climb ?—
        Nay ! Nay ! This cannot be !

I knew creation as a thought,
When suns and seraphim were nought,
Ere God's first fiat woke eternity :—
Below all gulfs beneath, beyond all heights above,
I know what being's sum wrecked, lost, could ne'er disprove,
I know creation's corner-stone is Love ! [1]
I know that GOODNESS *is man's final good,*
Pure loving goodness, like, from, in, his God ;—
Brave, humble, fruitful, all-enduring, sweet,
Goodness made his, love orbed in him complete.
This gift to man I bring.
This is the holiest thing
His soul can know, his being bear or borrow.
This lights his darkness, glorifies his sorrow,
Refines his spirit past all Art's adorning,
Illumes his reason with celestial morning.
‘   This solves life's tearful history,
And death's cold fearful mystery,
And flings o'er ruins wild and dread abyss
The beacon splendors of immortal bliss.
Mourn not that all terrestrial fades and flies ;
Doubt not that goodness lives, though nature dies.
Seek not my works, but ME.[2]
I AM THY DESTINY.

[1] Psa. 104 : 24, and throughout.
[2] " For she [Wisdom] is the brightness of the everlasting light, the unspotted mirror of the power of God, and the image of his goodness," etc.—WISDOM OF SOLOMON 7 : 26-30.

I fill infinity,

And rule eternity,

And gave myself for thee ;

And he who builds pure love on God's own love,

As o'er a drowned world safe, flew Noah's dove,

O'er seraphs lost, and suns in blackness driven,

Shall mount with song, and find God, Love and Heaven.

DE PROFUNDIS VIA CRUCIS: AN EXPERIENCE IN THEODICY.[1]

PART I. PRELUDE.

I.

OUT of the depths by the way of the cross !—

I mused on man's grandeur, his ruin and loss,

That problem of evil all ages have pondered,—

Saints trusted with awe,—sages questioned and wondered.

[1] This poem is what its title purports, a product of personal subjective experience, of the intensest sort, in every line.

As early as my reading and pondering over the profound problems presented in the books of Job and Ecclesiastes, in boyhood, and of Milton, in early youth, in a new settlement in Ohio, though I was then in active and (I believe spiritual) church membership, the great questions of the origin of moral evil, and the possibility of reconciling its existence with the divine perfections, began to burden my mind with increasing weight, that finally became at times an anguish almost insupportable. I found no satisfactory help from friends or books, though I read and questioned much, and I groped thus for about ten years. When studying metaphysics in my senior year in Columbia

II.

I mused till the anguish of millions was mine ;
Prayed, wrestled, and groped for the secret divine ;
Debated with schoolmen, vexed science and seers,
Then bowed, like blind Samson, in fetters and tears ;—

College I first became aware of the magnitude of the questions I was grappling with, and of the mighty minds that had dealt with them. But I got but little help from Leibnitz or his school of thought, or from several midnight conferences with some of the ablest divines and thinkers I knew. At last, on February 8th, 1861, while walking home from college, down Fifth Avenue, having just passed Madison Square and Twenty-third Street, as suddenly, and almost as overwhelmingly, as the light from heaven flashed upon Saul on the road to Damascus, the whole theory of the theodicy contained in this poem burst upon my mind, and I wept and shouted the praises of God on the spot. With a soul all ablaze I rushed to my room in Ninth Street, and in three and a half hours I had twenty-six stanzas of this poem on paper. Twenty-four stanzas were published, under the title of "*Optimum Omne*" (Everything Best) in the *Christian Advocate* of March 21st, 1861 ; and I immediately received many communications from thoughtful and intelligent persons expressing great mental and religious help received from the poem. It was also quoted in some religious and theological works of the times, and reprinted in various publications.

A second edition of the poem, under its present title, expanded to forty-one stanzas, appeared in the *National Repository* for May, 1880. Accompanying it my very learned and admired friend, Dr. Curry, the editor, printed the following editorial note, which I append here, reluctantly on account of its complimentary character, but of necessity because I desire to briefly reply to it. Dr. Curry said, on page 480 of the magazine for 1880 :

"It is not necessary to call attention to Dr. G. L. Taylor's poem in our present number, for it will surely sufficiently attract the attention of every thoughtful reader. It is a production of the class of Pope's ' Essay on Man,' where the vehicle of verse is used to transport a very heavy burden of solid thought, by which, indeed, the special poetical excellences of the vehicle may be concealed by the superincumbent mass of deep philosophy. It will, however, be found decidedly readable, and also thought-provoking. We do not, however, for a moment accept it as solving the profound problems with which it

III.

Sank ! tost and o'erwhelmed in doubt's whirlpool untold,
A maelstrom more awful than Norway's of old !
Till, praying, like Jonah, beneath the abyss,
In numbers I prayed, and the burden was this :

deals.   In his failure, however, the writer has an abundance of distinguished companions, among whom are such philosophers as Leibnitz and Bledsoe, and such poets as Pope, and Goethe, and Shelley—not to name the author of ' Bitter-Sweet'—and of learned divines ' a very great multitude.'   All these have by turns tried their hands upon the weighty theme, and, like the suitors with the bow of Ulysses, each has in turn failed in his efforts : though, somehow, each seems to have thought that he had hit the mark.   Milton makes the discussion of these points the pastime of the lost spirits.   Perhaps it would be wise to leave it to them.   No doubt, God's ways are all right ; they are also ' past finding out,' and all our theodicies are superserviceable attempts to justify the divine dispensations in a court before which he refuses to plead."

Thanks to Dr. Curry for his complimentary attack.   It is not strange, however, that he could not "for a moment accept" my humble effort as the solution of the "profound problems" in hand.   The poem was not written as an ambitious attempt at any such solution, but as the record of one soul's *experience*, for other like souls who might possibly be helped by it.

But the attempt to reconcile predestinarian theology with optimistic theodicy has made the production of a satisfactory theodicy impossible to many a great mind besides that of Leibnitz, and probably will ever do so.   Nevertheless, no soul of man upon whom these great "problems" have ever dawned will ever *rest* without *some* solution of them.   *Ignoring them* is *not* rest, and predestinarianism makes God a monster, while, on the other extreme, universalism makes chaos of divine government.   Neither gives a rational rest.   The agony is as old as the moral universe.   The author of the apocryphal book, II. Esdras 7 : 46–48, exclaims : " I answered him [God] and said, This is my first and last saying, that it had been better not to have given the earth to Adam : or else, when it was given him, to have restrained him from sinning.   For what profit is it for men now in this present time to live in heaviness, and after death to look for punishment ?   O thou Adam, what hast thou done !   for though it wast thou that sinned, thou art not fallen alone, but [also] all we that come of thee !"   These are some of the bottom ques-

PART II. THE PROBLEM OF THE AGES.

IV.

What is it to be ?—What is it to be ?—
Forever to drift o'er a limitless sea,
Still lost in a trackless and infinite haze
Of glories that dazzle, and doubts that amaze ?

tions of theodicy, echoed from the long ago. These questions will not be rel-
egated to the "vasty deep," nor to the debating clubs of pandemonium, at
the beck of even my revered friend Dr. Curry. Indeed, he seems to have forgotten his Milton, when he quotes him on this point. It is not theodicy, but
predestination—the antithesis and stumbling-block of all theodicy—which
forms the theme of Milton's fallen angels, who

> "reasoned high
> Of Providence, foreknowledge, will and fate ;
> Fixed fate, free will, foreknowledge absolute ;
> And found no end, in wandering mazes lost."
> —"Paradise Lost," Book II., lines 558–561.

That was only the logical result of predestinarianism, and of the *lack of
theodicy!* (My friend, Prof. B. P. Bowne, the eminent metaphysician of
Boston University, who saw this note, suggested that "the debate on Predestinarianism was a part of the punishment of the lost angels !" That view
would add new terrors to perdition !) But away with the idea of an irra-
tional theology ! God is the Infinite Reason. and he says to us, "Come,
now, and let us reason together !" (Isa. 1 : 18, R. V.) The blazing joy of a
reasonable faith is the sunrise of the soul ! But Milton's own view of theodicy is exactly the opposite of this suppression of reason in religion—nay,
theodicy is the very object he has in view in writing his sublime poem, Dr.
Curry to the contrary notwithstanding. In his opening Invocation he prays
for the Holy Spirit's inspiration :

> "That to the height of this great argument
> I may assert Eternal Providence,
> And justify the ways of God to men."
> —Book I., lines 24–26.

V.

Unending existence ! How awful ! How dread !
My soul shrinks appalled, and I cover my head,
As being's vast mystery looms on my thought,
Eternal, avoidless, unshunned, and unsought.

VI.

I scarce had dared ask so tremendous a dower ;
'Tis mine, by the fiat of infinite Power :
I tremble ; 'tis on me ; I cannot expire,
Nor 'scape from existence,—nor dare I desire.

That expresses the very idea and *word* of theodicy, which means the *Justification of God.* And probably the most successful and influential theodicy ever written is this same sublime " Paradise Lost," published over forty years before the " Theodicée" of Leibnitz. Milton's true theodicy is to be found in Book III., in the address of the Father to the Son concerning man's foreseen course, whom he had created :

" Sufficient to have stood, though free to fall,"

line 99, and in Book IV., in Satan's apostrophe to the sun, and soliloquy on himself, lines 32–103, a passage as awfully truthful in theology as it is sublime in poetry.

If Milton had more fully discussed the abstract and universal principles necessary to the existence, or even the idea, of moral righteousness and virtuous merit, and had not himself been somewhat entangled in predestinarian views, his great work would have been as impregnable as a theodicy as it is sublime above all other human compositions as a poem. The brief limits of this poem restrict me to a few of the central and fundamental ideas of the subject, the very ones which struck my mind like a blaze of light and joy, when the poem was first conceptually born, and written in outline, twenty-four years ago.

VII.

'Tis on me !—and with it the sin it has brought !
A crime past conception ! A woe beyond thought !
Launched forth on a life which no ages can span,
Yet orphaned from God since the ages began !

VIII.

No wrong had been done had my soul never been ;
No joy had I lost, and committed no sin ;
No Paradise forfeited, vengeance incurred,
No excellence blasted, nor holiness blurred.

IX.

But O, to go back into nothing again,
To a soul that has been, were more awful than pain !
To be blotted from being, engulfed in the void,
Were worse than despair of a heaven once enjoyed !

X.

I start back aghast from oblivion's verge
But to writhe on barbed sorrows, like lances that urge
My maddened soul forward to plunge the abyss,
And yet I shrink back from that horror, on this !

XI.

And this strife unending ! A soul self-abhorred,
Pursued by the wrath of an infinite Lord !
No price for a pardon, by pain or by pelf ; ,
No flight from perdition, but flight from myself !

XII.

No flight from the universe stained with my sin,
From vengeance without and from vengeance within !
From the infinite law, all-enduring and strong,
From the guilt, and the shame, and the ruin of wrong !

XIII.

" SIN !" blazes in wrath on the universe walls,
" SIN !" moans evermore through mind's innermost halls ;—
One groan from creation sin's agony tells ;
All worlds are polluted—all heavens are hells ! [1]

XIV.

O Father omnipotent, all thrones above,
Can this be my doom, and thy nature be LOVE ?—
No choice in my being, no choice in its end ?—
Can goodness and justice thus fearfully blend ?—

XV.

O Father, unfold this inscrutable plan !
O, save me from cursing the Maker of man !
Though banished forever from glory above,
Let me know that the law of existence is LOVE.

[1] " Me miserable ! which way shall I fly
    Infinite wrath and infinite despair ?
    Which way I fly is Hell ; myself am Hell ;
    And, in the lowest deep, a lower deep
    Still threatening to devour me opens wide,
    To which the Hell I suffer seems a Heaven !"
—*Satan's Soliloquy on Mt. Niphates,* " Paradise Lost," Book IV., lines 73-78.

XVI.

Let me know that in righteousness nature was planned,
And sin was no part of God's work or command ;
Or hail to old Atheism, Chaos, and Night!
Since right must make God, or no God can make right!

XVII.

My sin I confess, and its punishment due,
'Twere better I perish than God be untrue : [1]
I justify this : but, if destined to fall,
Why did He, who knew this, create me at all?

XVIII.

Foreknown is not fated, I see ;—should my choice
Have been free to be, or to not be ?—No voice
Can come from nonentity, God must decide,—
Deny me existence, or make, and provide.

PART III. THE DEBATE AND DECREE IN ETERNITY.

XIX.

Lo, infinite Righteousness, Wisdom, Power, Love,
Propounding the problem of being, above ;—
God, space, and duration,—alone and immense,—
No matter, no spirit ;—void—silence—suspense !—

---

[1] Rom. 3 : 4.

XX.

"If goodness and wisdom create, what they do
Must be holy and wise and beneficent too ;
It could not be other, *good cannot do ill,*[1]
Nor can it be *passive*, and be *goodness* still ;—

XXI.

The power to do good, unexerted, is ill ;[2]
Exerted, this infinite void it must fill
With good like itself, not in rank, but in kind,
With being, and beings, with spirit and mind.

XXII.

Diversity, too, must be part of the plan,
For goodness must flow through all forms that it can,
Or the good is not infinite ; hence every grade
And mode of existence, for good must be made.

XXIII.

But good must be free, or it cannot be good ;
No virtue in yielding what can't be withstood,
No worthy obedience where law is too strong,
No praise for the right, where there cannot be wrong.

XXIV.

Hence goodness demands that each rational mind
Have in its own structure, unforced, unconfined,

[1] Gen. 18 : 25.   [2] Jas. 4 : 17.

The power to originate evil, and sin
Unfettered, untempted, ere good can begin.

XXV.

Nor is this misfortune to him, but his right,
His being's perfection, his gate to delight,
His excellence godlike, that gives him the power,
Unfallen, to merit his heavenly dower.

XXVI.

And what though, in rashness and folly, some world,
Some order celestial, from glory be hurled ;
Their sad lapse shall prove the high freedom we gave,
And call forth new wonders to rescue and save.

XXVII.

But some, lost forever, may shoot the abyss
Of infinite evil ; like planets that miss
Attraction and orbit, quit order's bright shore,
And darkle down gulfs below gulfs evermore.

XXVIII.

All this, in its dread possibility, waits
The word that one moral immortal creates !—
But myriads on myriads wait being and bliss
From the fiat that starts such a spectre as this !

XXIX.

Yet being were better than never to be,
And being were noblest, intelligent, free ;

And knowledge and freedom, with evil foreknown,
Were better than blind brute-existence, alone.

XXX.

Yea, being *must* be, since, though evil befall,
Far vaster the evil, no being at all ;
Then God were the sinner, small evil repressing
By great, by withholding the universe-blessing.

XXXI.

Creation *must be*, where Creator has trod ;
No infinite good, then no infinite God !
No infinite Fount without infinite flow !
No infinite good without possible woe !

XXXII.

Yea, *all* lost, for aye, *still* creation were good !
Still Reason adores, and Right justifies God !
'Twixt universe empty, or universe lost,
Right claims the great chance,[1] with its gain—or its cost !

XXXIII.

This is no dilemma, but infinite sight
Discerning the only, the absolute right ;
And infinite Reason demands right be done ;—
" LET THERE BE !"— And there *was*—and creation begun !

---

[1] The term "chance" is here used in its old English sense of *opportunity*, that chance to earn reward by merit which even an uncreated universe would have the right to demand of One with infinite power to create.

XXXIV.

That fiat, impulsive, smote deep through the void,
And space flashed with sundrifts, like armies deployed :
Force, matter, mind, spirit, from monad to man,
And all the bright complex of being began.

PART IV. THE ASSENT OF REASON TO THE LAW.

XXXV.

O, Father Omniscient, Abyss of pure love,
Perfection ! Perfection !   Beneath and above !
Perfection ! Perfection !   All, *all* things done well ! [1]
Perfection forever, in heaven, earth, and hell !

XXXVI.

A world without freedom, from evil restrained,
Were a world barred from virtue, an universe chained !
And though freedom fall, and from virtue be riven,
No possible hell, were no possible heaven !

XXXVII.

Aye nethermost hell's ever-deepening abyss
Attests highest heaven's ever-heightening bliss ;
By moral, eternal necessity thus ;
As infinite minus proves infinite plus !

---

[1] Ps. 104 : 24 ; Mark 7 : 37.

XXXVIII.

Aye infinite hell proclaims Infinite Love
Not less than the blaze of all glories above !
In love God created, compelled by its power ;—
In love he gave freedom :—heav'n, hell, are its dower.

XXXIX.

O Father of Mercy, forgive thy rash child,
Gone wild in rebellion, in anguish gone wild !
My being was infinite goodness expressed,
I never can curse thee, for once I was blessed.

XL.

I never can curse thee, though down the dark steep—
The madness of evil unending—I sweep ;
The great *gifts* of being, power, freedom, were *thine*,
The *choice*, sin or virtue, shame, glory were *mine*.

XLI.

I never can curse thee !   Thy goodness shall shine
Through worlds and eternities, damned or divine !
One arch of perfection thy universe stands ;
One temple of Righteousness, built by thy hands !

XLII.

Below all abysses rock-founded its piers
On Righteousness rise through eternity's years !
Above all abysses, all heavens above,
Its pinnacles soar in the light of God's Love !

XLIII.

And in this dread temple, which compasses all,
Abashed and o'erwhelmed as a sinner I fall!
Guilt! Guilt! Vile ingratitude! Foulness abhorred!
"Hell"? Hell were a refuge from heaven and its Lord!

XLIV.

Aye, hell were a refuge from Purity's sight!
From Love long insulted! from Mercy's despite!
Wide, wide throw thy portals, O Gulf beyond name!
I plunge, self-condemned, and self-damned, to thy flame!

XLV.

I plunge!—But what cover were hell, from that eye
Of Mercy, long-outraged, whose glance I would fly?
Hell scoffs at my madness, confesses its Lord,
Lies naked before him, and quakes at his word![1]

XLVI.

The walls of the universe fence me with fire!
Its dome is one EYE! an eye blazing with ire![2]
Existence is anguish! Immortal! Undone!
Non-existence abhors me! On! On! Ever on!

XLVII.

On whither?—O whither, for refuge from SIN!
Hell blazes without! and hell blazes within!

---

[1] Job 26 : 6.   [2] Ps. 139 : 7-12.

Wretch !   What were hell's pit to the soul's own dread pyre ?
Eternally chained to a conscience on fire !

XLVIII.

Woe !   Woe to the soul that hath sinned against light !
Against God, self, the Universe, Reason, and Right !
Still Righteousness reigns, but for me is the glare
And the gloom, of the gulf of eternal despair !

PART V.   LOVE VICTORIOUS IN REDEMPTION.

XLIX.

O Father of Mercy, what now do I see ?
God-Christ !   God in man !   He is dying !   For me !
O infinite tenderness ! stronger than death,
My life his last heart-throb, my name his last breath !

L.

" Forgive them !"   " 'Tis finished !" he murmurs, and dies !
Earth reels in amazement !   Night mantles the skies !
All nature avows him !   The dead quit the grave !
He dies ; but he rises, the " MIGHTY TO SAVE !"

LI.

From Edom he cometh,[1] in vesture of blood !
From Bozrah he marches in strength like a God !

---

[1] Isa. 63 : 1–6.

Law's wine-press of wrath he has trodden alone !
Love's year of Redemption dawns bright from God's throne !

LII.

Lo ! through those five rents in the veil of his flesh,
The Godhead within him outblazes afresh !
Wrath ! wrath against sin ; but the love that can die
With joy, to save sinners, illumes earth and sky !

LIII.

Hail, thorn-crowned Redeemer ! My sad, bitter heart
Breaks down, mercy-melted ! My frozen tears start !
My dark doom was just ; this is mercy alone,
Such mercy as none but my God could have shown !

LIV.

My Substitute there in that Victim I see ;
The wrath that o'erwhelms *him* had else o'erwhelmed *me !*
He pays my last debt, blots the page with his gore,
And the stained sword of justice gleams lightnings no more.

LV.

He stands with the arms of his mercy outspread !
He bids me accept him who died in my stead !
Thrice damned be my pride, if such love it repel !
The pride that scorns love were too hellish for hell !

LVI.

O Lover ! I perish ! I fly ! I embrace
My death in thy dying ! my life in thy grace !

New power to hate sin, and new power to love good,
Stream flooding my soul with the rapture of God !

LVII.

The *Rapture of Righteousness !*   Righteousness *mine !*
Imparted, *inwrought,* by a wonder divine !
Faith's miracle perfect !   New-born and forgiven !
Cleansed ! Justified ! Sanctified ! Hell changed for heaven !

PART VI. POSTLUDE.

LVIII.

Sin's riddle is ended.   Doubt's problem is clear.
Earth, heaven, and hell, are all justified here.
Yea, let God be righteous, though man's be the loss ;
Down gulfs and abysses light streams from the CROSS !

LIX.

From gulf and abyss by the cross I ascend.
There hangs my Redeemer, my Judge, and my Friend ;
My ransom, my cleansing, my joy evermore ;—
I gaze in rapt wonder, and love, and adore.

LX.

I gaze without terror, where angels with awe
Desire[1] to look into Love's infinite Law ;

[1] I. Peter I : 12.

Where thrones [1] and dominions God's wisdom shall learn !
And cherub and seraph with new rapture burn !

LXI.

I gaze without terror.   From Eden the sword
Departs, and Earth hails her Shekinah [2] restored.
God shines through all souls, through all worlds that obey ;
And the light of his smile is Love's infinite Day.

LXII.

Now glory to God, to the Father, and Son,
And Spirit, thrice worshipped, the THREE in the ONE !
Praise, honor, and blessing !   Shout angels again !
All worlds, hells, and heavens, shall echo AMEN !

A METHODIST CENTENNIAL SONG.

[Delivered on several occasions in connection with the celebration of the First Centennial of American Methodism, in 1866.]

THOU, O all-inspiring Spirit ! all-illuming, unconfined,
Deep from out the inmost ardors of the calm, eternal Mind,
Breathe on us thy fiery effluence, those who hear, and him
    who sings,
Flash through every soul thy fervors !   Waft us all on rapt-
    ure's wings !

[1] Eph. 3 : 10.
[2] Gen. 3 : 24, the shekinah, before which men worshipped, is undoubtedly expressed in the imagery of this verse.

Ere from godlike bliss Edenic lured and hurled by hosts of
    hell,
Man, the favorite of Jehovah, like a new-born planet fell,
In the counsels of creation, ere the endless silence heard :
" Let there be !"—and worlds from nothing rolled harmoni-
    ous at the word ;—
There, ere eldest archangelic orders hymned the wondrous
    plan,
Yearned the undiscovered Godhead with the love that died
    for man :
Yearned, and when he fell proclaimed it in that promise faint
    and far,
Glimmering down Earth's twilight distance like a dim and
    misty star.
Down long prehistoric ages, down the patriarchal years,
Dawned its beams on saints and sages, rose on raptured bards
    and seers,
Till, with one wild burst of anthems warbling through a thou-
    sand spheres,
Lo, Immanuel, Everlasting Saviour, Prince of Peace appears !

Day immortal ! Day uncelebrated still, though Earth so
    long
Beats and pants with pulse seraphic, soaring up the heights of
    song !
Not by mortal lays, and not by all the ecstatic choirs above,
Ever has been, ever shall be told Redemption's depth of
    love.

As the broad, bright tides of morning stream o'er Ocean's
    boundless breast,
As from out the East the lightning shineth even to the West,
So, through every land and language to the known world's far-
    thest bound,
Flew the glad news of salvation and the long-lost Eden found !

  Wondrous then the change transforming hearts and nations
    in a day !
Men, to moles and bats their idols casting, owned Messiah's
    sway ;
Art, philosophy and learning, song and science, power and
    fame,
Thrones and kingdoms, mightiest empires, all adored Imman-
    uel's name.

  Then, alas ! a wave of midnight o'er the troubled nations
    spread ;
Manhood failed and Freedom perished ; learning, science,
    song were dead ;
And the great salvation, bought for man with agony divine,
Bound, blasphemed, was sold for lucre, bartered at an impious
    shrine !

  Lo, once more celestial sunrise wide o'er Earth in splendor
    plays !
Gloom and error flee before it, smit with Truth's resistless
    rays !

Rack and dungeon, axe and fagot, all in vain its light with-
    stand ;
God's almighty love must conquer,—who can bind Jehovah's
    hand ?
Wickliffe, Huss, Savonarola, Calvin, Luther, Cranmer rose,
Wrapped in zeal like Israel's prophets when they pled with
    Israel's foes ;
Rending off the soul's base bondage, long in blood and vileness
    trod,
Pointing faith alone to Jesus, conscience only to its God.

Then, with vast and wondrous quickening, lo ! the mind of
    man awoke !
Nations started from their slumbers as at midnight thunder-
    stroke !
Seas were crossed, new worlds discovered, stars unknown from
    darkness swung !
'Round the globe the shout of progress rang through every
    land and tongue !

Then, ah ! then a cloud of evil, scoffing, doubt, dispute, and
    sin
Veiled the brightness of the dawning, shut the heavenly sun-
    rise in ;
Wrapped in shade Immanuel's standard, late o'er longing
    lands unfurled ;
Damped the fire on Zion's altars, dimmed her light that lights
    the world !

But not thus could fail God's promise, purposed ere the world
    began,
Breathing, burning down the ages unextinguished love for
    man :
Not one jot or tittle written ever from his law shall fail ;
'Gainst the Church, by Jesus planted, gates of hell shall ne'er
    prevail.

  Lo ! Immortal WESLEY, scorning ease and pleasure, honor,
    fame,
All his mind on fire from heaven, all his heart with love
    aflame,
All his ardent soul illumed, anointed with the Holy Ghost,
Sanctified and sealed, arises, called to lead the blood-washed
    host !
Called to preach the great salvation, boundless, endless, full
    and free,
Grace that saves man's utmost being, saves through all eternity!

  Thousands caught the rapturous tidings ; heard, believed
    with shouts of praise ;
Spread from isle to isle the story, set Britannia in a blaze !
O'er three thousand miles of ocean winds and waves the mes-
    sage bore,
Like a spark from heaven falling, kindling on this NewWorld's
    shore !
Here awhile, repressed, it smouldered, till, by God's own
    Spirit fanned,

Glimmering, rising, spreading, mounting, soon it swept o'er all
the land !

First in *Barbara Hick's* pure spirit leapt to life the long-
pent gleam ;
Swift from soul to soul it lightened, darting wide its dazzling
beam,
Till, as flames o'er autumn prairies fling their banners fierce
and high,
Mingling in a fiery ocean flashing earth and glowing sky,
So the chariot of Jehovah, wrapped in brightness, as of yore,
In a pentecostal whirlwind swept the infant nations [1] o'er !

Embury and *Webb* and *Strawbridge* first the lambent tongues
confessed ;—
Owen, Williams, King, and *Watters, Boardman, Pilmoor,* heroes
blessed;—
ASBURY, the great Apostle ; *Whatcoat, Rankin, Shadford, Lee ;*
Abbott, Garretson, and *Coughlan, Neal, M'Geary, Black, Losee ;*
Wooster, Poythress, Cooper, Dickens, George, M'Kendree, Roberts,
Cook ;
Emory, Hedding, Fisk, and *Olin, Bangs,* all graved in God's
great book ;—
Names illustrious as their labors ;—deathless as the march of
time ;—
Bright with undecaying glory—sainted, high, serene, sublime!

_____

[1] Infant nations, *i.e.* the colonies.

Then rose venerable " JOHN STREET," and " SAINT GEORGE'S "
    ample shrine,
Altars where God's own Shekinah burned with ceaseless light
    divine ;
Where the living word, like lightning, fell from fire-touched
    lips of old,
And the shouts of new-born thousands heavenward like an
    anthem rolled !
Not alone the blissful baptism Wesley's favored followers
    knew,
O'er the land, their flaming herald, matchless, wondrous
    WHITEFIELD flew ;
Every priesthood, creed, and order owned the impulse, proved
    the power ;
Far and widening spread the influence, deepening, heightening
    every hour.

Next came war and revolution.   Strife and uproar shook
    the land ;
Leagued oppression toiled to conquer Freedom's young heroic
    band ;
But Jehovah, God of battles, saved the weak but smote the
    strong,
And a NATION rose victorious, hailed around the world with
    song !

Then, with her, a CHURCH as mighty called her heralds from
    afar,

Chose her chiefs, and rose organic,[1] marshalled for a heavenlier
war :

" FREE GRACE," " FREEDOM," " FULL SALVATION," on her blood-
stained banner flew ;

And around the cross she wrapped the starry flag—red, white,
and blue !

True to man, and true to Jesus, panoplied in light she
stood ;

Heaven to her one hope for all men, man one blood-bought
brotherhood.

" HOLINESS UNTO THE LORD " and " PERFECT LOVE " illumed
her van ;—

Thus complete her march triumphant down the centuries
began.

Then what future lay before her, save Jehovah who could
tell ?

What her agonies and conquests, how her gathering hosts
should swell,

Till, to-day, the shouts of millions shake the earth and cleave
the sky,

Echoed back by millions ransomed, warbling through eternity !

On, through storms that rocked the nations, bold she held her
glorious track,

Grandly stood for God and justice, cast no glance of trembling
back ;

[1] Rose organic, when the Methodist Episcopal Church was organized, at
Baltimore, at the " Christmas Conference " of 1784.

And when Slavery's vast rebellion rose, insane with Treason's
    ire,
Up she sprang a harnessed seraph, bright with keen celestial
    fire !
Where the foremost ranks of Freedom, winged with wrath, to
    victory rode,
There the cross above the eagle like a meteor gleamed and
    glowed !
And among the faint and dying walked sweet Mercy's angel
    bands,
On their lips the love of Jesus, life and healing in their hands.

  Lo, the giant conflict ended ! Slavery's shackles rent in
    twain !
Righteousness and Peace, embracing, soon o'er all shall smile
    and reign !
Millions kneel on fetters broken, bathe with tears the blood-
    dyed sod,
Shout their anthems throbbing up the sunlight of the throne
    of God !
Stretch their anxious arms imploring for man's rights with-
    held so long,
Asking only light and justice, fearing only hate and wrong.

  With the nation's joy exultant, lo ! anew the Church up-
    springs,
Fired with purer, loftier rapture, while a holier joy she sings !
Wesley's children, myriads, millions, bless with transport and
    with tears

Him whose grace has brought them victors through a hundred
    deathless years !
Thronging now in thousand temples glad they bend the ador-
    ing knee,
Pealing high their great CENTENNIAL, thundering forth their
    JUBILEE !
On their century's latest confines peering backward in amaze !
Forward on a future grander than e'er greeted prophet's gaze !

    Church of God, what wonders wait thee in that future hast-
    ening near,
In this New World's vast arena, noblest empire on the sphere !
What thy myriads who can number ? How thy greatness yet
    shall mount ?
What thy work, thy trust stupendous ? Who can sum the
    dread account ?
Deep in utmost, sweet abasement mourn thy sins, forsake,
    abhor ;
Claim thy spotless robe, and wear it ; rise, already con-
    queror !
Pile thy gifts like golden mountains ! Heap thy holocausts
    untold !
Bid the spires of countless temples tower toward heaven while
    time grows old !
Build thy schools for unborn prophets ! Rear thy halls of
    hallowed lore !
Let long-distant generations bless their sires who wrought
    before !

Aid thy struggling sons whose souls, on fire with Heaven's
    resistless call,
Grope through nameless want and heart-ache toward that sun
    which shines for all !
Send thy light to those in darkness ! Save thy children ! Save
    the poor !
Broadly sow beside all waters ;—God shall make the harvest
    sure !

  Living temple of Jehovah, precious in thy light most
    clear,
Framed to mock hell's hate, upsoaring till thy dome shall roof
    the sphere,
Not in mortal might nor wisdom lay thy deep foundations
    low ;
Not in earthly pomp and grandeur let the wondrous fabric
    grow.
On the Rock of endless ages bid thy crystal turrets climb,
Gold and jasper, emerald, diamond—stones of truth to last
    through time !

  Israel's God, we bow before thee ;—all our inmost souls we
    bow ;—
Take our prostrate hearts and treasures :—seal our consecra-
    tion now !—
Let the rushing, fiery whirlwind, as of old thy Spirit came,
Fill thy temples—fill the children—crown thy Church with
    tongues of flame !

Up, O Zion!—Tell the story!—shout the tale to millions
    dumb!
God is risen in glory on thee!—Rise and shine, thy light is
    come!

GRACE TRIUMPHANT.

["My grace is sufficient for thee."—PAUL, II. Cor. 12 : 9.]

Dedicated to the Methodist Itinerant Ministry,

BY ONE OF THEIR NUMBER,

who can say with John: "I . . . , your brother, and partaker with you in the tribulation and
kingdom and patience *which are* in Jesus, was in the isle that is called Patmos, for the word
of God and for the testimony of Jesus."—REV. 1 : 9, R. V.

I.

'TWAS an hour of the dread power of darkness [1] and doubt ;
Sore trials encompassed my pathway about ;
Wrong triumphed ; betrayal, opprobrium, shame,
Injustice, dishonor, were heaped on my name.

II.

The hopes, toils, and rights of my life overthrown,
In the prime of my manhood I stood stripped and lone ;
Peeled, outraged, and exiled, my life's sun seemed set ;
Earth lay a black desert 'neath heavens of jet.

[1] "This is your hour, and the power of darkness."—Luke 22 : 53.

III.

Then, crushed, half heart-broken, I cried to the Lord ;
I fainted, fell helpless, but fell on God's word ;
When, out of the darkness, a voice spake to me,—
" My grace is sufficient—sufficient—for thee !"

IV.

Half startled, yet cheered at that voice clear and strong,
Like the voice of a friend 'mid a strange, taunting throng,
I groped till the record through tears I could see,—
" My grace is sufficient—sufficient—for thee !"

V.

And then I read onward, where glorious Paul
" As a fool "[1] tells his conflicts and triumphs o'er all :
" In toils more abundant, in stripes, prisons, chains,
In deaths," yet he glories, and never complains.

VI.

" Five times, forty lashes save one have I owned !
I was thrice bastinadoed, and once was I stoned ;
Thrice shipwrecked, a day and a night in the sea,
But his grace was sufficient—sufficient—for me.

VII.

" In journeyings often, from parishes chased
Where sin reigned defiant, and Christ was disgraced ;

---

[1] Read II. Cor. 11 : 16 to 12 : 11.

In perils of robbers—yet robbers were tame
To saints who assassinate truth and good name !

VIII.

" In perils by countrymen, city, and waste,—
Ah, bitter the sorrow when trust is misplaced,—
But ah, by false brethren deserted to fall,
Is bitterest, shamefulest, saddest of all !

IX.

" And yet will I glory, nor weakness, nor want,
Infirmity, poverty, peril, shall daunt ;
Let down in a basket by night though I flee, ,
God's grace is sufficient—sufficient—for me.

X.

" Sometimes to third heavens translated I rise,
And visions of Paradise ravish my eyes ;
Revelations unspeakable over me roll,
Transporting, o'erwhelming sense, body, and soul !

XI.

" And then Satan's messengers buffet afresh,
And rankle like thorns in this passionate flesh ;
But when to the Mighty in anguish I flee,
He answers, ' My grace is sufficient for thee !

XII.

" ' My strength through thy weakness made perfect shall shine ;
Thy sorrows, reproaches, distresses, are mine ;

Christ crucified walks among men in thy shame,[1]
Christ crucified, wearing thy form and thy name !

XIII.

" ' Canst lend me thy name ?   Is't too precious for me ?
Canst lend me thy form ? that once more men may see
Their Lord, in thy likeness, and own me, confessed
Meek, pure, patient, brave, in my servant distressed ? ' "

XIV.

Then, sudden, my sad, sinking heart felt a shock,
Like falling in dreams—but my feet struck the " ROCK " !
My soul sprang exultant !   Grief's nightmare was flown !
And Christ, like the sun, through Paul's sorrows outshone !

XV.

Hail, Hero for God !   What were my wrongs to thine ?
Yet smitings and shames were thy laurels divine !
Persecutions, necessities, obloquy, scorn,
They melt at thy ardor like mists of the morn !

XVI.

Then hail, Hero-Spirit !   A joyous All-Hail !
Though storm-clouds may gather, life's hope seem to fail,
So Christ stand beside me, whate'er can befall,
I'll triumph, O Master, with thee and thy Paul !

---

[1] " Always bearing about in the body the dying of Jesus, that the life also of Jesus may be manifested in our body."—II. Cor. 4 : 10, R. V.

XVII.

A "fool," too, *I'll* glory in stripes for thy cause,
For loyalty true to thy oath and thy laws ;
And when foes assail me, and coward friends flee,
Thy grace shall suffice me—I'll suffer with thee.

XVIII.

I'll suffer with thee, ever-crucified King ;
Defeat has no bitterness, Death has no sting,
While thy smile from heav'n's crystalline wall beams to me,—
"My grace is sufficient—sufficient—for thee !"

XIX.

Thy witness, I'll stand, 'mid earth's smile or its frown !
Thy banner, O Captain, I'll *never* haul down !
Though I fall at my post, this my death-song shall be,
God's grace is sufficient—sufficient—for me !

XX.

O Rest ! sweet, sweet Rest ! Love's victorious Rest !
O Conqueror, thorn-crowned, I lean on thy breast !
There's heav'n in that whisper—thy whisper to me,—
"My grace is sufficient—sufficient—for thee !"

WORK IN REST.

I.

AH me, how vast is the boundless space !
  Ah me, how long is the endless time !
  How sweet, how holy the psalm sublime
That floats, as balm from a crystal vase,
From all that is, to the heavenly place.

II.

How sweet, how holy that ceaseless psalm !
  It melts and sinks through the depths above,
  Fainting like pulses drowned in love,
Dying, like zephyrs in groves of palm,
Or the inward flow of the tide's full calm.

III.

How smooth, how calm are those star-sprent planes !
  How calm are the drifted worlds that stream
  The ether oceans with foamless gleam !
A benediction of calmness reigns
Through being's illimitable domains.

IV.

There is no hurry in all the skies ;
  The fret and flurry of finite years,
  The heats of spirit, the worry and fears,

And the tears that bleed from our human eyes,
  Are all unknown in those unknown spheres.

V.

So smooth, so still, through the stormless deep,
  Unchafed by ripple, unrocked by tide,
With a patient, tireless, majestic sweep
  Through the long, bright lapse of their years they glide,
And yet their changeless sereneness keep.

VI.

There is no heat, no hurry in heaven ;
The living creatures, the spirits seven,
  The prostrate elders who next adore,
  The millions who chant on the amber shore,
  Are calmed with rapture forevermore.

VII.

God never hastens. Through all the deeps
  Of the Goodness infinite, teeming still
  With ever-creative thought and will,
And the patient care all being that keeps,
The calm potential and blissful sleeps.

VIII.

For God, the All-worker, works in rest ;
  Out of his nature creation grows,
  Out of his being all being flows,

As the rivers from Eden, unrepressed,
Boundless, exhaustless, beautiful, blest.

IX.

And deep through the unknown, soundless sea,
   Outward forever, on every side
   The spheral waves of his effluence wide
Vibrate through shoreless infinity,
   Filled and filling with life as they glide.

X.

And the vibrant thrill of that boundless Life
   Is the measureless, ceaseless pulse of Love ;
   All-blessing, beneath, abroad, above,
With sumless, blissful beneficence rife,
Too wise for sorrow, too strong for strife.

XI.

And up to that Infinite Life and Love
   The endless cry of creation goes ;
Million-voiced, dumb, at the Heart above
   It knocks, till the answer all worlds o'erflows
   With love that lightens and glory that glows !

XII.

O Infinite Energy, born of Repose,
   Repose, of Infinite Energy born,
   Unspent, serene as creation's morn,
   My restless spirit, toiling and worn,
In the restful might of thy being inclose.

XIII.

O Thou, the All-worker, work in me
  Thy patience, purity, power and peace !
O clear my vision thy purpose to see,
Work in me and through me, that I in thee
  May rest and work, with eternal increase.

THE LIGHT OF THE WORLD.

'Εγώ εἰμι τὸ φῶς τοῦ κόσμου.—JOHN 8 : 12.

I.

LIGHT of the Kosmos, Reason, Cause
  Of all that is, below, above,
    Centre and spring of Life and Love,
And Lord of Love's eternal laws ;

II.

One world of thine we dimly scan,
  And own it full of wrong and woe ;—
  We know not why it should be so,
Nor why should sin thy offspring, man.

III.

We know we sin. Through mind and heart,
  Through soul and sense defilement stains ;
    The good in us is bound in chains
Whose links we will not rend apart.

IV.

And darkness, vast and dense and sad,
  Hangs o'er us all, a tearful cloud ;
  Each heart with aching throbs aloud,
With none, none, none to make us glad.

V.

What, none ?— Nay ! nay ! O Thou Divine !
  Thou Light of Worlds ! We see thee stand
  'Mid suns abashed on either hand,
O'erawed we see thee stand and shine !

VI.

Thou shin'st for us ! In mortal frame,
  With mortal weakness compassed 'round,
  In thee, and thee alone were found
Love's spotless light and scathless flame !

VII.

Thou shin'st in us. Truth's crystal ray
  From thee, thyself, the Truth who art,
  Fills Reason's eye and Passion's heart,
And lifts us toward thy nameless day.

VIII.

Thou shin'st through us. From man to man,
  From age to age, from race to race,
  Thy broadening beams our darkness chase,
To crown with light what light began.

IX.

As Truth and Love took human mould
　To touch and teach and save at first,
　So still, from soul to soul, as erst,
Must goodness win its way, and hold.

X.

Our goodness Thou, our love and light,
　In us set up thy kingdom soon ;
　Shine, shine to boundless, blissful noon,
To noon that knows nor shade nor night.

XI.

Like sunrise lances through a wood,
　So through our hearts, through nations, climes,
　Flash, till the clash of heavenly chimes
Shall hail o'er earth the dawn of good !

XII.

Rise, orbed in glory !　Saviour !　King !
　Jehovah !　Jesus !　Truth !　Light !　Love !
　Lion of Judah !　Lamb and Dove !
Reign Thou, till earth like heaven shall sing !

IMMORTALITY.

When I behold the ocean, mountains, sky,
The broad, green prairie, rimmed with heaven's own blue,
The white cloud-ships that sail the summer noon,
The midnight's awful dome, on fire with stars,
And drink the rhythmic silences that steal
Solemn, eternal, through the universe,
My spirit pines with longing to explore
This stream of boundless being to its Source,
To find its far, unfathomed, central Spring,
The Nile-fount of existence, Godhead's sea,
Shoreless abyss of conscious life and love,
Whose spheral waves of force creative sweep
Vital, unspent, widening eternally,
Breaking to song and star-foam as they roll.

And I have felt within me strength to roam
Though galaxies and glories, far beyond
These realms of order into eldest night ;
Beyond attraction's reach, or light's last gleam,
Through outer emptiness, where height nor depth,
Substance, nor centre, nor circumference,
Obstruct the spirit's flight ;—for rest to poise

On crags of solid darkness ; or, unchilled,
On wing to plunge the fixed and sensible gloom
Through gulfs where order's wide and fair domain
Shrinks to a sand-shoal, lost in tideless seas ;
Where ancient Chaos' old atomic wars
Ne'er stirred the atomless void of nothingness ;
Where space is all ; where time ne'er was, event,
Nor date to chronicle eternity.

    And when my soul, like one long pent in towns
But now glad wandering wide o'er breezy hills,
Had stretched her powers in grateful exercise,
And roomy freedom, then 'twere joy to turn
From this abysmal, void infinitude
Toward the far coasts of day. Intuitive,
Past hells and limbos, steer on steady wing,
To where, faint glimmering down the dusk expanse,
One tremulous beam points out a universe,
A point, perspective, widening, breaking bright,
Until the glittering maze of wheeling orbs,
Suns guiding suns and worlds convoying worlds,
Once more in tuneful march should 'round me roll.

    And I have longed attraction-winged to voyage
Studious, through starry archipelagoes
Of drifted clusters, all compact of suns,
A luminous labyrinth, tow'rd that globe unknown
Whose vast convexity the centre fills,

A steadfast sphere, unmeasured, unrevolved,
Broad as Sol's wheel among morn's blinking stars.
Far up its golden tides of primal dawn
Eager I'd sail, while soft prismatic floods
Of rosy effluence streamed through sense and soul,
With rhythm harmonious as the cadenced close
Of angel vespers round the twilight throne.
Were I unfleshed, this hour my soul should spring
O'er that far flood, to find its fountain clime,
And scale its cataracts, cliffs diaphanous,
Of lucent flash, poured from the mount of flame,
Crystal Olympus, throne of Him whose feet
Set Sinai altogether on a blaze.

I shall behold them.   Can a being die,
Conceiving thoughts of immortality ?
Shall I all perish, when this frame dissolves
Back to its fellow-elements, rebuilt
Mayhap in thousand forms, while ages roll ?
Can this self-conscious, personal *I* expire,
A wreck of outworn tissues, forces spent,
Spent or transformed, a chemic drop sublimed ?
Is this what roams the stars, and talks with God ?
Avaunt vain babblers, philosophic fools !
God is ! I am ! and while he lives I live !
Nor shall this wondrous body, all forgot,
Want essence and resemblance, though transformed
Ten thousand times, through twice ten thousand years.

E'en these were but as moments.   Earth grows old,
And rocks, unsteadfast, on her axle worn,
Shuddering through all her blind and stony frame,
With secret dread, her chronologue of doom.

And let that moment speed : let long-pent fires
Rend and enwrap this dull material ball,
Brighten then blot this planet in its turn,
And strow its cinders through the darkened sky ;—
They have done this before, and shall again,
For He who bids them burn still bids them build ;—
They cannot scathe the soul, nor scorch its wings.
Entire, immortal, undissolved, serene
I shall ride upward on th' exploding flames
That warp and crack the firmamental spheres [1]
And shrivel yon blue heaven like a scroll,—
Shall find that stainless city, built by God,
Whose four-square walls, from rainbow quarries hewn,
Whose streets of lucid gold, whose diamond domes,
Stand, while the white throne lights the universe.

O Thou, Almighty, thy creating breath
Could scatter all these systems thou hast framed,
And chase the nebulous drifts of starry dust,
Planets, and satellites, and clustered suns,
Driven like the chaff of summer threshing-floors

[1] The crystalline spheres in the ancient Ptolemaic system of the universe.

When western whirlwinds mow the woods, and strow
With wrecks of ruined villages the plains,
And scourge the yeasty cauldron of the deep
Till watery Andes whelm the shuddering shores !
Terror and glory, majesty and love,
Alike are thine, alike divine and good.
These shall not harm nor fright a child of thine,
For thou hast breathed that same immortal breath
Into these moulds of clay, and sealed it here,
With all its prisonless energy and fire,
To warm these breathing clods,—but not forever.
Deep from eternity a whisper comes,
Stealing like melody through all our being,
That tells us of a large and free existence,
A life unlimited, in which the flights
And voyages of imagination here
Shall be the soul's experience, not her fancies,
Her glad, intelligent travels, not her dreams.

APPENDIX A.

CHRONOLOGICAL TABLE OF CONTENTS.

Title.	First writing-place.	Date.	First publication.	Date.
The Incarnation. Part I. A Christmas Carol.	Medina (Lenawee Co., Mich.), Union Seminary (extinct).	Dec. 25, 1853.	New York, *Independent*.	Dec. 23, 1880.
The Incarnation. Part II. The Magi.	Medina (Lenawee Co., Mich.), Union Seminary (extinct).	Dec. 25, 1853.	New York, *Christian Advocate*.	Dec. 16, 1880.
Immortality	Ohio Wesleyan University, Delaware, Ohio.	March 19, 1858.	" " "	Feb. 5, 1874.
Destruction of Egypt's First-Born	Ohio Wesleyan University, Delaware, Ohio.	Oct. 12, 1858.	New York, *Independent*.	Nov. 8, 1860.
Passage of the Red Sea	Ohio Wesleyan University, Delaware, Ohio.	April, 1859.	New York, *American Monthly*.	Jan., 1861.
The Smiting of the Rock in Kadesh	Columbia College, New York.	Oct. 27, 1860.	" "	Dec., 1860.
De Profundis Via Crucis	" " "	Feb. 8, 1861.	New York, *Christian Advocate*.	March 21, 1861.
The World-Wide Hope	" " (Junior Exhibition).	Feb. 13, 1861.	New York, *National Repository*.	May, 1880.
Armageddon	Columbia College.	May 13, 1861.	New York, *Excelsior Magazine*.	June, 1868.
A Vision of the Ages	" " (Graduating Poem.)	June 26, 1861.	New York, *Christian Advocate*.	Aug. 8, 1861.
			Cincinnati, Ohio, *Ladies' Repository*.	Jan., 1863.

Title	Place	Date	Publication	Publication Date
Proem—"Non Nobis, Domine,"	New Britain, Conn.	July 30, 1864.	New York, *Christian Advocate.*	Dec. 15, 1864.
Work in Rest	" "	Oct., 1865.	New York, *Scribner's Monthly.*	May, 1872.
A Methodist Centennial Song	Brooklyn, N. Y.	June 18, 1866.	New York, *Harper's Weekly.*	Oct. 6, 1866.
The Light of the World	" "	Feb. 9, 1867.	Boston, *Zion's Herald.*	July 10, 1867.
Elijah the Reformer	" "	July 11, 1870.	Delivered, Wesleyan University, and elsewhere.	July 10, 1870.
The Scourging of Heliodorus	Hempstead, L. I.	July 7, 1871.	New York, *Tribune.*	Aug. 30, 1871.
The Prophecy of Wisdom	" "	Aug. 28, 1871.	Delivered, Cornerstone Laying, Syracuse University.	Aug. 31, 1871.
The Sacred Glory of Old Age	" "	Sept. 15, 1871	Proem for 8vo vol., "Threescore Years and Beyond," by W. H. De Puy, D.D., Carlton & Lanahan, New York,	1872.
Paul at Philippi	" "	Jan. 5, 1872.	New York, *Christian Advocate.*	March 28, 1872.
The Christmas Bells	" "	Dec. 25, 1873.	New York, *National Repository.*	Jan., 1878.
The Calling of Moses	" "	Jan. 8, 1874.	New York, *Independent.*	Jan. 22, 1874.
Grace Triumphant	Torrington, Conn.	Jan. 19, 1879.	New York, *Christian Advocate.*	April 3, 1879.
The Sword of the Lord and of Gideon	Ridgefield,	Aug. 3, 1881.	" "	July 12, 1883.
Faint yet Pursuing	"	Aug. 6, 1883.	" "	Nov. 20, 1884.
Jehoshaphat's Deliverance	"	Aug. 12, 1883.	New York, *Independent.*	Sept. 13, 1883.
The Passage of Jordan	"	Dec. 3, 1883.	New York, *Christian Advocate.*	March 27, 1884.
The Overthrow of Jericho	Brooklyn, N. Y.	Nov. 23, 1884.	" "	May 28, June 4 and 11, 1885.
The Fiery Furnace	" "	March 28, 1885.	Boston, *Zion's Herald.*	June 10, 1885.
Elisha's Fiery Chariots	" "	May 12, 1885.	Cincinnati, Ohio, *Western Christian Advocate.*	May 27, 1885.

www.ingramcontent.com/pod-product-compliance
Lightning Source LLC
Chambersburg PA
CBHW021048030726
47496CB00006B/1739